BENJAMIN, MY SON

BENJAMIN, MY SON

GEOFFREY PHILP

PEEPAL TREE

First published in Great Britain in 2003
Peepal Tree Press
17 King's Avenue
Leeds LS6 1QS
England

ISBN 1 900715 78 3

Grateful thanks to Robert Pinsky and his publisher for
permission to quote from his *The Inferno of Dante: A
New Verse Translation* (Noonday Press)

LIVICATION

The book that you are holding in your hand is a miracle, so give thanks to the Creator of all miracles.

Give thanks to the elders and ancestors: my mother and father, who taught me about loving and letting go; my teachers in the flesh: Dennis Scott, Mervyn Morris, Kamau Brathwaite, Martha McDonough, George Lamming and John Hearne, who one rainy afternoon in the Extra-Mural Center (UWI-Mona) taught me *how* to write fiction; the teachers who've inspired me: Derek Walcott, Pablo Neruda, Tony McNeill, Joseph Campbell, William Faulkner, Flannery O'Connor, J. California Cooper, Edgar Mittelholzer, Sam Selvon, Zora Neale Hurston, James Baldwin, Orlando Patterson, Roger Mais, James Joyce, Gabriel Garcia Marquez, and, yes, V. S. Naipaul.

Give thanks to my friends who have stood by me in the past two troubling years: Josett Peat, Lou Skellings, Lisa Shaw, Florentino Gonzalez, Colin Channer, Preston Allen, Edwidge Danticat, Mervyn Solomon, Kwame Dawes, Gina Cortes, and Susan Orlin; Erika Waters and the staff of *The Caribbean Writer*, Janell Walden Agyeman of Marie Brown Associates, Mary Luft of Tigertail Productions, Pastor Annette Jones and Carol Hoffman of St. John's on the Lake; Victoria Kupchinetsky of PEN whose generous grant helped with this and many other projects; and Hannah Bannister and Jeremy Poynting of Peepal Trees Press who continue to create miracles for so many Caribbean Writers.

Finally, give thanks to my family: Paco, abuelo, rest in peace; Anatolia, abuela, the matriarch; Tathi and Batsheva, my sisters; Frank, my idren; Judith, Winsome, Dicky, Ansel, Paul, Hal, Madge, Heather, Stephanie, Cherrie, Edison, Ronald, Debbie-Gaye, Ricky, Terry and Kerry—it finally happened!

For Nadia, my traveling companion; Anna, Andrew and Christina, for all the years of laughter, tears and joy, give thanks, give thanks, give thanks.

Follow me and I will be your guide
Away from here, and through an eternal place:

To hear cries of despair, and to behold
Ancient tormented spirits as they lament
In chorus the second death they must abide.

Canto I, *The Inferno of Dante*
Trans. Robert Pinsky

"A house divided against itself cannot stand"
Mark 3:25

CHAPTER ONE

"Bumbo," said Trevor, and he moved closer to the television. "Jason, you've got to see this, man. What the hell's happening in Jamaica?" The camera probed the silver edge of the tide. "Move closer, man, you've got to see this."

I wasn't usually interested in what Trevor watched in the afternoons, especially before our Wednesday night domino tournaments. Oprah and Court TV had him hooked. If he couldn't find anything interesting on either channel, he switched to CNN. It really didn't matter to me what he watched. What mattered was that we won all our games and picked up a little money along the way, for we had become local celebrities at Churchill's, our favourite bar in Little Haiti.

"Turn it up! Turn it up!" I said. "That's Dada!"

The scene on the television resembled something out of Rwanda or Haiti. The streets were littered with corpses that had been covered with newspaper while the police and itinerant mad men stared implacably at the cameras and shooting continued in the background. I could almost smell the bodies, necklaced with tires, burning in the middle of Kingston – the black smoke coiling lazily over the cobalt blue waters of the Caribbean Sea.

"Although one of the assailants, Desmond Russell, political henchman for the PNP, was killed in self-defence by Albert Lumley, Minister of Justice," said the CNN reporter as he loosened his tie, "it appears that the other assailant or assailants are at large. Some suspect it was a drug-related murder. Others suspect political motives. David Carmichael, leader of the PNP, whose headquarters have been firebombed, has called for calm. In the midst of this unrest, the Prime Minister has declared that the state of emergency will not interfere with the upcoming cricket test match between the West Indies and England. The start of the match, however, will be delayed until Saturday..."

Gina, the waitress on the night shift, came in from the kitchen. She was a small woman with a leathery tan, raven black hair and a broad gap-toothed smile, but she also had a stare that could cool down the most hotheaded patron and sober them up immediately.

"You know that man? I'm so sorry to hear," said Gina.

"Don't be," I said. "It was only Dada. *El padre putativo.*"

Dada. This was the first word my mother taught me – even before she taught me her own name, and before she slipped off to America to forget him. And I know why. As soon as I had sense enough, I hated him, too. Hated him for what he had done to my mother, hated him for what he had done to me, hated him for what he had done to that beautiful, damned island.

No wonder I kept ending up in these dead-end bars. I looked up at the nets above our heads and across to the west wall that was decorated with scenes from the Everglades: ospreys and egrets in the gnarled limbs of cypresses, alligators lolling in the river of grass. Above the mural, a blue marlin suspended over the cigarette machine gathered dust on its dorsal fin. In front of me, a heron was harpooning a rat snake, and under its wings an octopus was mired in murky ink, shifting its shape and colour in an aquamarine haze.

An ad for a new barmaid was plastered over the jukebox.

"Watch it with the *puta* business in here," said Trevor and slipped a coin into Galaxomaze, a video game he played whenever he was nervous. "Gina runs a respectable bar," and he winked at her.

Dressed in black and wearing his favourite T-shirt – one of the many he'd won at Churchill's for drinking every brand of

8

beer in the bar – his war uniform as he called it – Trevor was ready for the domino tournament that night.

At thirty-five, six years my senior, Trevor was a thin gangly man with bulging eyes, a scraggly goatee, and a bad temper. He had promised me earlier that he was going to send every double, including mine if I was careless, to the bone yard. "Call Range Funeral Home!" he shouted, waving his hands in the air like an obeah man exiling unclean spirits, before he slapped down the killing card, "This one's going straight to Woodlawn!" I reckoned we would win about a hundred to two hundred and fifty dollars that night, and I needed it.

I gazed at the screen and watched the most recent videos of Dada campaigning at a political rally. Twirling his hands in the air and snapping his fingers like a whip, he was coaxing the crowd into a frenzy and railing against the curse of drugs – his lifelong mission. Some women at the front of the stage tried to reach for the cuff of his pants as if he were some aged televangelist stalking the stage for converts.

One woman leapt on the stage and kissed him full on the lips (security around Dada was always lax when it came to women), but his bodyguards soon dragged her off. Dada, without missing a beat, continued his speech. He clearly enjoyed the encounter and he was glowing. I always imagined he would die from a heart attack in the arms of some girlfriend who wanted more than his mind after he'd given one of his famous speeches. But murdered, I thought, even Dada didn't deserve to die like that.

"So who's that?" Gina asked pointing to the television.

"That's my big brother, Chris," I said and I touched her hand, trying to reassure her I was okay. "He'll probably be taking over everything."

"That's your brother? He doesn't look anything like you." I think she was surprised that I was taking Dada's death so coolly, but she didn't know Dada.

"You meant darker, didn't you?" said Trevor.

"I meant different," said Gina. She glanced at Trevor. "You know, I don't deal with that shit. Never forget that," she said

9

sternly and picked up a mop she had left by the freezer. Pine Sol smothered the smell of Tuesday night.

Gina was very sensitive about skin colour and Trevor should have known better. Gina's friends often teased her about her twin sister, Lily, the *negrita*, who was a shade darker than she was and who walked around Miami with packets of charms and oils in the waist of her dress. Lily, unlike Gina, was not ashamed of practising Lukumi, or Santeria as her gringo friends called it. Gina visited the *babalao* only when things were bad and she couldn't turn anywhere else. She reminded me of Dada's friends, who after climbing out of poverty and ridding themselves of what they saw as superstitions, still went to an obeah man if things were spinning wildly out of control.

"I'm sorry," said Trevor.

Trevor had already cleared the first three levels of the game and had chosen a light sabre as his weapon, but he was caught in a black hole that reduced the screen to a pinpoint of light. His craft veered off course, wheeling and tumbling through the gravitational pull of a small moon, a coin trailing a spire of flame through the stratosphere, and crash-landed in the lunar dust.

"So how come you never told me about him?" Gina asked.

"Not you, but I told Trevor and Nicole about him. And he's really my half-brother by my father's first wife."

"Jesus!" she said. "How many times was your father married?"

"Three times and with several mistresses and girlfriends in between."

"So do you have any other brothers you haven't told us about?" Gina asked.

"No, I'm my mother's only son."

"I mean by your father," she said.

"Stepfather," I reminded her.

"Whatever," said Gina.

"I don't know." Who could tell with Dada?

"I know what you mean," said Trevor, his Honduran accent slipping. "I know what you mean."

10

Trevor was trapped between dimensional strings, would take some time before the machine decided on level he would find himself. Pulling back on his bar stool, started humming, "Papa was a Rolling Stone", and I hit a high five with him. Gina turned away from us.

Trevor and I both hated our fathers. His father, like a good many Caribbean men, had fathered several children in and out of wedlock. He also beat Trevor's mother regularly. When Trevor was old enough to defend his mother, his father threw him out of the house.

"I can't believe you're acting this way, Jason," said Gina. "Your father just got killed!" and she turned off the television. She walked along the counter, stacked a few dirty dishes, and then went back to the kitchen. "I'll be in the back if you need me. I'll get the Red Stripes for tonight."

"Why's she taking it so badly?"

"I guess she misses her father in Cuba," said Trevor. "He's sick and she feels guilty about leaving all her family behind. But she's more worried that she may be tempted to chuck it all and go back to Cuba. But enough of that. When do you want me to pick you up to go to the airport?"

Brandishing his light sabre, he defended himself against a snake woman who had emerged out of the dust and wrapped her tentacles around his ankles.

"Where am I supposed to be going?"

"To the funeral," he said. "I know how you feel about him, but you have to go to his funeral."

"And why is that? Have you forgotten what he did to my mother? He's the one who broke my mother's heart and killed her."

"Jason, she died from pancreatic cancer."

"That's the medical name for it. But you know the real reason she died. She didn't deserve to be abandoned for her own cousin. Why should I honour a man like that?"

"Because you need to," he said. "He's the one who brought you up."

That was the only reason I could think of to attend his

funeral. He had brought me up, but I figured it was only out of guilt because he had abandoned my mother.

"Just because I lived under his roof doesn't mean he owned me. He could never understand that with all his power, he could never control me. Did I ever tell you he tried to get me to change my name from Stewart to Lumley?"

"No," said Trevor.

"Yeah," I said. "Just before I came to Miami to live with my mother, he asked me to change my name. When I came to America, I decided to put him and all that behind me. Because of him, I wanted nothing to do with the island. That's why I became an American citizen. I even have a passport to prove it."

"A passport doesn't prove shit. If anything it makes it more important for you to go to the funeral."

"Going to the funeral won't solve anything. It will just make matters worse. There are too many people down there that I don't want to see. Not now. Besides, most Jamaican men don't know their real fathers, so why should I go back for a dead stepfather?"

Trevor was thrown into the dungeon of the overlord, Galaxomaze. The beast sidled up to him and chewed off his arm. He was losing power.

"And that place," I said. Trevor braced himself for my favourite litany that I counted out on my left hand, "It's just full of people who lie and are dunce, lazy, slack, and arrogant."

Trevor shook his head and twirled his mug of beer making the frothy head rise to the top.

"Well, at least toast the motherfucker," he said. "I'm not playing with you or drinking with you until you toast him."

"Okay," I said. "To Albert. Rest in peace. Now drink up."

"I've never turned down a beer in my life," said Trevor. Which was true. Trevor had never turned down any drink or drug in his life. Ever since he was dishonourably discharged as an army medic, he'd done every drug on the planet: ice in Seoul, LSD in Chicago, heroin in LA and crack in Miami. I've never met anyone so obsessed with his own destruction and who pursued his goal with such diligence.

And like all addicts he always claimed he could quit at any time and if things got too bad, he'd take the cure – rehab. And things weren't going well. His ex-wife was remarrying.

Trevor swivelled on the barstool and opened the pouch around his waist. He looked around the bar, glanced over by the door, and showed me a spliff he'd tucked away in the lining.

"Got some good herb today. You got to try some of this. It's from your hometown. Good Lamb's Bread, bro. With this herb I'll be able to see right through the dominos. You gotta smoke some with me, bro."

"For the millionth time, Trevor, I don't smoke the stuff any more."

I'd stopped smoking herb a few years ago. I'd bought a nickel bag in the Grove and went back to my apartment to get high and watch The Three Stooges. As I lit up the spliff, I flicked on the TV and there was a graphic report on a DEA agent who was tortured and killed by drug traffickers. I saw his remains being loaded into the back of a pickup truck and I couldn't take another draw. Every spliff in America was tainted with his blood.

"Yeah, yeah, I know. You only smoked it with your Rasta brethren. What were those guys names?"

"Papa Legba and Reuben."

The names alone brought back a torrent of memories. When I turned twenty-one and couldn't take it any more in Albert's house, I wandered around the island for about three months before coming to Miami, wandering around as aimlessly as I was doing now. I spent most of the time with Reuben and Papa Legba, the Rasta elder who renamed me Benjamin, according to the calendar of the Twelve Tribes of Israel.

"Papa Legba, that's the name I liked," said Trevor. "He must have been able to get his hands on some good weed. You know you're the only Jamaican I know who doesn't smoke weed."

"It's the company you keep. And they've been teaching you too many bad words."

"What the raas do you mean by that?"

"See what I mean."

"Well," he smiled, "if you're not going to smoke, at least walk with me," he said, and swallowed the rest of the beer. Trevor had defeated Galaxomaze by using his own power against him. He was about to rescue the alien princess, but hesitated at the door. The old star fighter had lost his nerve. He ran towards the alien princess and she plunged a dagger in his chest. Game over.

"Okay, I'll walk with you. The cops have been sniffing around here."

"Fucking cops," he said, "why don't they just let us be? We're already cornered here in this rat hole. What more do they want?"

"See, that's just why Gina wants me to walk with you. She doesn't want any trouble with you and them."

By the look on his face, I knew I'd struck a nerve. But I hadn't meant to.

"She said that? She had no right to say that, bro! She had no right to say that," and he raised his voice so that she could hear him. "I'm so pissed I might take my business to another bar where I won't be insulted."

"Take it easy, Trevor. She heard you. She heard you."

"I don't care if she heard me. She insulted me, bro. I'll go somewhere else. I will."

"She doesn't mind you smoking, but do it as far away from the bar as possible. She likes you. You're one of her best customers."

"I'll say. I already owe her next week's paycheck." He lowered his voice. "Tell her I'll have the money for her by next Friday."

"I know you will," I said and I wasn't patronizing him. Trevor was the best telemarketer for our company NileSource Inc. If Trevor really put his mind to selling four hundred units, he could do it. A few years back, he'd been the vice president of Thaganana Limited in the Cayman Islands, but he smoked the company into bankruptcy.

I still hadn't learned all of Trevor's tricks, though he had been guiding me since we first met up four years ago. In that first telemarketing job, I was assigned as his junior partner and he stood up for me in the first few months when I was struggling to meet my quota.

"He'll come along," said Trevor, and I never let him down. So when a senior supervisor fired Trevor for drinking on the job, this supervisor and I almost came to a fistfight, but I fooled him with my best yardy accent:

"Is blood claat fight, yu want? I will fuck yu up you know, boy!"

It had been a long time since I'd been in a fistfight and fortunately he got scared and backed off. Score one for the yardies. I left the job and we both went to work with at NileSource Inc., which paid better. I'd even been able to save some money, and was planning to take a vacation in Jamaica and look up Dada. I wanted him to see that although I'd dropped out of college, I'd made something of myself. Maybe then we could talk.

But my mother's death put an end to that. After several costly misguided diagnoses, her health insurance was capped off at a hundred thousand dollars. I still owe Jackson Memorial, where she worked as a private nurse, twenty thousand dollars for her initial care at the hospital. I had to sell her house to pay for a condition that proved to be terminal. "Always keep property," Dada advised, "no matter what." I used all the money I'd saved to give her a decent funeral. It wiped me out. However, I refused on principle to take any money from Dada. I didn't want to owe him anything.

Trevor stuck by me all those times. He took me in after I had moved from apartment to apartment to apartment and when I was homeless for a while. He got me drunk when I needed to get drunk, and kept me sober when I had to be. Trevor even lent me some of his clothes, mainly T-shirts, some of which I kept long after I moved out of his place.

But now I was in more financial problems. Our company was in a slump and we were laying off workers. Some were leaving on their own. Trevor and I had been below our targets for three months and we were barely hanging on to our jobs.

The only reason our boss kept us on was that he knew we were good and couldn't be blamed if people didn't have any money. I needed to pay the rent, my student loan, Visa, and MasterCard bills. Calls from my creditors were coming in at all hours of the night and morning. I hated owing anyone anything and I could feel the frustration rising in my temples every time the phone rang. Sometimes, I just let the phone ring without checking the caller ID, sometimes losing a call from Nicole, my girl-friend. But I lived in constant fear of the bill collector and the repo man.

Right now, the rent was the most important because if I didn't come up with the money, I'd be on the street again. I knew I could always stay with Trevor, but Nicole didn't like going over to his place because Trevor was a slob. Always hungry, his apartment floor was covered with boxes from Papa John's Pizza, Suzy Lai's, or Hammond's Tasty Flakes.

"So how are you going to break this news to Nicole?" He rubbed his finger against his wedding band.

Sometimes I don't know how we ended up being friends; our minds work so differently when it comes to important matters. Trevor had been divorced for eight years, but he never took off his wedding band. The minute I got divorced from my ex-wife, Simone, I pawned my ring and I came to Churchill's to celebrate my own liberation day. I played a game of pool with him and we've been friends ever since. Churchill's became our sanctuary against all that was happening outside. It was unaffected by the race riots swirling around Miami. Here we could sit and have a drink in peace without anything disturbing us.

"We had another argument," I said.

"Whatever it is, apologize and buy her flowers. I learned the hard way not to fight with women."

"That's why I need some extra money," I said. "I am going to buy her some flowers. Her father was over at her apartment and we got into an argument."

"About what?"

"Besides the fact that he says I'll never amount to anything,

16

he also found out that I supported David Carmichael when I was in Jamaica."

"Who's that?"

"He was once the Prime Minister and her father was one of those who feared that Carmichael would introduce communism into the island. Her father lost everything, and blames it on Carmichael. He's an ex-cop and he's trained his dog, King, to shit whenever he says Carmichael's name."

"You really are in the crapper," Trevor said. "But don't let something this small come between you," he said. "That's nothing if you really love her. You do love her?"

"Yes," I said. That was about the only thing in my life that I was certain about. "But I'm not certain we want the same things."

"Give yourselves time," he said. "Nicole is a good woman. You should hang on to her no matter what."

"But, Trevor, what can I offer her? She has this great job and a great future and look at me. What do I have to offer her except words?"

"Sometimes words are all you got, bro. Do you know how many situations I've had to talk myself out of? And if you're so strapped for money, why don't you just swallow your pride and go down to Jamaica. Or are you still too proud to beg? What is it with you Jamaicans? If my old man dropped dead tomorrow, I'd go see if he left me any money in his will."

The thought had crossed my mind.

"Why would he leave any money for me?"

"You never can tell," said Trevor. "Just because of your stubbornness you could be cheating yourself out of your inheritance. Give up some of that pride they taught you in that 'English' boarding school you attended. A little humility could solve all your money problems."

Trevor was right. Despite my doubts about going back, even the remotest chance of an inheritance was worth the trip. I needed the money.

We pushed away our mugs and stepped out of the bar into the night air. I looked away to the lights from the Haitian

Marketplace. A jitney crawled by, bumping over the potholes and splashing through the dirty water to pull up by the bus stop. A woman in a tight floral dress that barely covered her buttocks got out and a man called after her, "Cherie, take me home." She pulled down her skirt, turned, and in a second was gone. The jitney trundled on.

A barefooted man was ambling unsteadily up the street, evidently drunk. As he passed, he bumped into me, staggered backwards and held on to the side of the building for support.

"Beg your pardon, boss," he said, "beg your pardon." He looked at me from behind a mat of hair that arched upward from the top of his head, then curved down to cover his face. I thought I recognized him, but a crust of grime covered his forehead and twisted Raybans shielded his eyes.

"Spare a dollar, boss?"

I reached in my pocket and gave him a dollar. Trevor kissed his teeth. The man took the money, gave me a drunken blessing, and continued up the road.

"Motherfucker, I can't believe you," he said. "You don't have a pot to piss in, but you're giving money away."

"There but for the grace of God is what my mother used to say."

"You one crazy nigger," said Trevor.

Winston Churchill looked down on us from the bar sign and flashed his famous symbol across Miami. We were waiting for the light on the opposite side to turn green when Trevor dashed across the lane and I followed him. He slipped his hand into the pouch and pinched out the spliff from the lining. He palmed the spliff and headed across the yard to a tool shed we'd discovered one night when we couldn't hold down any more beers. It was covered with a web of philodendrons and honey-suckle and was invisible from the street. Here, Trevor could smoke his spliff in peace.

Trevor looked up and down the road, then parted the vines to go through the door. As he cleared the leaves, a man emerged from inside with what looked like a crack pipe in his hand. He pulled a gun from inside his vest.

I couldn't run, so the minute I saw the gun I knocked it

away. Trevor hit him in the stomach and then across the temple and he fell. He was remembering all that they'd taught him in the army. The man's head hit the asphalt. Trevor turned him over to check his pulse and found a police badge inside his vest. He showed it to me.

"What are we going to do?" I asked.

"He's still alive, but he's going to need help. He's been smoking crack and his pulse is high. This concussion isn't going to help him either. You get the hell out of here. Get as far away from here as possible. This is serious shit, bro!"

"But I can't leave you here!" He was my friend. I wasn't going to leave him as I had left the others.

"You don't have a choice. This is serious shit. This is jail time, bro."

And that was when I panicked. I had once visited Trevor in the Dade County Jail when he was arrested for possession and distribution of crack, and I never wanted to go back.

Trevor had blown his entire paycheck on over thirty grams and had it stashed in his car when the police pulled him over, so they charged him with intent to distribute. He called me from the pay phone in the cell and Nicole and I went down to see him. We couldn't afford the ten percent premium to post bond for him because he was now being treated as a dealer. The humiliation of being searched, checked at every point and the sound, more than anything else, of those huge iron gates closing behind me, gave me nightmares for a whole week. I never wanted to go through that again.

"What about you?"

"Don't you understand? You can do all the drugs in the world, but you never hit a cop. Get out of here, bro. These guys, even when they're breaking the law, always have their partners near, so get out of here, fast."

"But..."

"Get the fuck out of here!"

Trevor lifted the cop over his shoulder and I took off in the opposite direction. I had barely gotten to the other side of the alley when I heard, "Freeze." I ducked down immediately and hid behind a dumpster.

"Freeze!"

"It's okay," said Trevor. "It's okay."

"Shut the fuck up and put him down!"

"It's okay," said Trevor. "It's okay."

"I said, shut the fuck up! Is there anyone else with you?"

Trevor didn't say a word. I peeped through the gaps between the houses. It must have been the injured cop's partner.

"Could you help me here," he said to policeman. "This guy's in trouble. I used to be a medic. I saw him when he fainted over there."

I didn't want to leave, but I had to. I turned, began walking down the lane, then a quick step, a jog, and then a full sprint away from the bar. I ran and I ran until I couldn't run any more.

I went straight to Nicole's apartment and hid out there. I didn't tell her what had happened with Trevor, but I did tell her about Dada's funeral. As I talked with her, I figured if I went down to Jamaica, my brother, Chris, with his connections in the government, could protect me from extradition or anything like that. Anything was better than Dade County Jail.

That night we started packing for Jamaica.

CHAPTER TWO

The wind ripped across the face of the flag flying at half-mast inside Jamaica College Cemetery that Friday morning. Green ribbons and placards – "Death to all PNP. Blood and Fire. Fire Burn PNP. Long live the JLP" – hung from the trees surrounding the cemetery and flapped furiously in the stiff breeze. In accordance with his last requests, Dada wanted a small service instead of an elaborate ceremony at the National Arena. But this was not to be. The small chapel on Matilda's Corner was crammed with people who had known and supported Dada over the years.

At least I was dressed properly for the service and hadn't broken any of the unwritten rules of protocol. We had rushed everything, and Nicole and I had barely enough time to pack all the things we needed. Nicole had to get a new dress and I had to get a new suit. By the time we'd finished shopping and bought our tickets, it was already Thursday afternoon. Luckily, because of all the commotion about the state of emergency, with the help of my brother we had managed to slip through customs and got home in time to get a good night's rest before the funeral. I'd even had time to check my voice mail at home and my office for any messages from Trevor. He hadn't called.

Now, afraid that I might draw undue attention to myself, I moved with Nicole into the transept away from the honour guard, teachers, and alumni of Jamaica College. Dada, my brother and I were Old Boys. Many in the Prime Minister's cabinet were Old Boys, as indeed were many of Jamaica's leaders. Friendships made there frequently endured through JC alumni's professional lives. We were expected to become part of what Dr. McClaren, our headmaster, stealing a phrase from W. E. DuBois, called "the talented tenth". We were expected to lead, to rule this island, and I was failing dismally.

During my years at Jamaica College, this church had been the safest place I knew, for it kept me away from my father's sordid world of affairs and politics. I had moved from choirboy to acolyte and my mother even thought I'd join the ministry, but life got in the way. Now I had to face everything on my own.

Women wailed as the priest intoned the last words of the order of burial: "Surely we brought nothing into this world, and it is certain we can carry nothing out. The Lord gave and the Lord hath taken away. Blessed be the name of the Lord. Amen."

The congregation responded and a volley of gunshots rang out from the trees. Nicole tugged at my arm, but no one – not the dons, gorgons and guinea gogs, linked arm in arm with the politicians, pastors and pundits – moved. They'd grown accustomed to these displays of grief from party supporters. No funeral was complete without a sharp burst of an Uzi to punctuate the mourners' sorrow.

The cameraman from JBC panned the mourners, and held on Nicole's face as she bowed her head, lost in her own private prayer. Her black dress, with silver lining around the neckline, accentuated her dark brown hair, olive complexion and the emerald green eyes that she had inherited from her great-grandfather.

The camera then swung around to the Prime Minister, and then to David Carmichael, the leader of the PNP. My brother, Chris, always the dandy, wore a brand new Armani suit. He stood out among the Old Boys with their dull blue blazers, the school insignia, *Fervet Opus In Campis,* embroidered across the pocket. Almost six feet tall, about the same height as Dada, Chris' eyes were set wide apart, and this often made him look as if he were going to break out in laughter at any moment. Now though, his eyes were squinted to slits and the bags underneath them showed his exhaustion as he lowered his head with senior members of the JLP as the casket was lowered into the ground. Chris had taken care of all the arrangements. And when he was too exhausted to carry on, he had been helped by Dada's lodge brothers, who were the pallbearers.

I waited until I thought the cameras were pointed elsewhere, then made my own gesture. He was dead. He couldn't hurt me any more. The new shirt I'd bought chafed my neck as I stared into the dark hole and sprinkled a handful of dirt over the casket. It had rained earlier so the dirt was cool and moist. A stone, hidden in the clay, thudded against the casket. My tie felt like a garrote.

The casket seemed too small to contain the man who had ruled my life for so long. The last time I had seen him was at the airport in Kingston. He had driven me there himself, and without his bodyguards. Emma, my stepmother, always got angry when he did this, but I guess he wanted to be alone with me. He hugged me in front of the customs officer, and I didn't know what to do, so I stood there until he let me go.

Now, Emma stepped in front of me to pay her last respects. She held herself erect, a graceful woman. She'd barely eaten since Dada's death, and all the brightness in her eyes that had endeared her to him had fled, and the plain black dress she wore made her cinnamon brown skin seem pale and lifeless. She looked around the cemetery, almost as if she was expecting to see her friend who, if he could have been there, would have made fun of his own death.

I could hear her whispering under her breath, "I miss you, Albert. I miss you. I can't do this alone. I can't. I need your help."

So far Emma had been brave and had stood up to the Prime Minister, who had posthumously bestowed on Dada, the title of OM, the Order of Merit, the third highest civilian honour. This caused a minor scandal because the opposition, led by David Carmichael, implied that his own colleagues were honouring him only after years of neglect, and that Dada preferred his other title of QC.

Emma stayed out of that battle, but she resisted the members of Dada's party, and Chris, who for political reasons, wanted to drag out Dada's funeral for a week. Emma limited the viewing to two days, despite the protests of the Old Boys and the party. It was an easier battle to win than it might have been, because they realized that they would be competing against the test match. They knew, loyal as Dada's followers were, that if faced with the choice between a cricket match and a funeral, there was no competition – and this was West Indies versus England. Everything would be shut down. Everyone would be hooked to their radios for the latest score. Banks, schools, garbage, everything would be on a go-slow, like the times of the famous labour disturbances that Dada led against Carmichael, forcing him to call early elections. Carmichael had been defeated and had not been in power since.

Emma bowed her head to acknowledge me, some of her black hair escaping from under her veil. I could smell the perfume she was wearing, Amarige. She was so weak she could barely walk. She threw a bouquet of chrysanthemums on the casket, lost her footing in the loose earth and would have fallen if her old friend, David Carmichael, had not caught her.

Although Carmichael was in his late sixties he still had an athletic agility. He was tall, with a high forehead and deep set eyes that were as black as ackee seeds. He still retained the shape of a sprinter's body, built for speed with no room for excess.

During my adolescence, he had been the only politician that I'd ever trusted. In a country that lacked living patriots, he had been a hero to my generation. A self-made man who had run a successful poultry business, he was drawn into politics out of disgust over the bauxite deals that his political predecessors had made with the multinationals. Either out of collusion, naiveté or stupidity, his predecessors had signed away Jamaica's mineral rights, so the island would never see one millionth of the profits that were being drained from it. What's more, the bauxite companies were leaving behind an ecological disaster that worsened soil erosion and muddied the coral reefs around the island. The multinationals would walk away when the bauxite reserves were depleted. And why shouldn't they? There was no EPA behind them, and it wasn't on American soil, so it was perfectly legal rape. Who would stop them, the same politicians who'd given our rights away?

Photographers from the *Gleaner* and the *Star* zoomed in on Emma in Carmichael's arms, and he released her as soon as she could stand on her own. She grasped the arm of his Kareba jacket and looked up at her old friend's face, creased from years of endless campaigning. The crowd was silent as Carmichael balanced her on his arm.

Chris burrowed through the throng of mourners, placed himself between Carmichael and Emma and very publicly brushed away Carmichael's hand. Carmichael, though visibly stunned by the force of the repulse, held back from any kind of confrontation. His friend and rival demanded more respect and he could see Emma was at breaking point, so he withdrew into the crowd.

Picking up another wreath in the party colours, Chris faced his supporters and threw it on the casket. More gunshots rang out. Chris had waited for and planned this moment and Carmichael had upstaged him. He held Emma's arm, shielded her with his body, and signalled to the gravediggers to begin their work.

Already tipsy from the over-proof white rum that Chris had given them, the gravediggers had been waiting as patiently as the statues surrounding the headstones. One of them was patting a dog on the head as it scratched around the graves. They scrambled around, but by the time they found their shovels, the military was ready to give the official twenty-one gun salute. The National Anthem followed and there was a moment of silence for Albert Lumley, QC, and OM.

As the mourners bowed their heads, a gap-toothed woman in a red sequined dress that was slit to her thighs broke through the crowd of mourners. The Prime Minister was whisked away in his limousine and soldiers with bared bayonets guarded his exit.

"Murderer!" she screamed and lunged at Carmichael. Jagga and Butto, Carmichael's bodyguards, crisscrossed in front of her when she pulled out a Coke bottle containing a yellowish liquid.

"Grab the bottle!" shouted Jagga. "Grab the bottle."

Butto wrested the bottle from the woman's hand, making sure not to spill its contents on himself or anyone else in the crowd.

"Is acid?" asked Jagga, before he shuttled Carmichael through the crowd.

"No, piss, and rank too," said Butto. The woman was handcuffed and led away by the police who pushed her into the back of a police car.

With the commotion that the woman caused, there was soon a traffic jam at the eastern gate. Nicole had left with Emma and her Land Rover was stuck at the southern gate. A few Old Boys, with whom I now had nothing in common except the old bully boy banter or, worse, aimless chatter about the good old days, were coming toward me and I made a beeline between the cars. There I spotted my old art teacher at Jamaica College, Basil Cunningham, getting into his old VW van. Who could miss him? Blind in his left eye – a congenital defect – and over six feet tall, he still sported an Afro and a spade-like goatee. He was taller than everyone else in the crowd, and his eye patch and flowing African robes made him all the more recognizable.

Basil was always my refuge from these bores whose only aim was to talk about the glory days of the college. I wanted nothing to do with them. Their lives were devoted to the ideals of the college, for which they would sacrifice everything. They had only a past; Basil was concerned with the future.

As I made my way through the crowd, I saw Verna, a former maid with the family, hobbling into a taxi with a woman who was about my age, whom I didn't know. I called to Verna, but she didn't hear me. I was about to run over to Basil's car when Larry Buchanan, "The Buckmeister" or "Bucky Marshall" as we called him, slapped me on the shoulders.

"Herbert Spliffington, you old raas."

I hadn't been called that name in almost ten years. It was the nickname Larry had given me when he found out that I and my bunkmate, Reuben, were going to Papa Legba's camp and smoking massive amounts of herb.

Larry, burly and bowlegged, looked like an English rugby player. His sandy blond hair, that turned green one summer because he was trying out for the swimming team, was never combed and drooped down over his gray-blue eyes. He was as sloppy as usual. His tie was knotted in his own peculiar design and his thinning hair showed streaks of gray.

He was the last person in Jamaica I wanted to see. Besides being the most fiercely political of our small group in high school, he was also the brightest. He had achieved everything that Dada had hoped I would have done: passed the SAT with perfect scores and been offered scholarships to MIT, Yale and Harvard, which he politely declined and went on to study at UWI. We always thought he was trying to live down the shame of being labelled by the communists as a member of "Thirteen Families" that supposedly controlled Jamaica's economy.

"So how are you doing?" he asked. "What are you doing now?"

"Marketing," I said, repeating my familiar lie. "And you?" trying not to give any hint of weakness, for he was so smart, he could weed out any inconsistencies and unravel the facade of success that I'd been trying to project. I wasn't going to admit to Larry or anyone that I hadn't lived up to what they had all expected of me. I had a lot to hide.

"I'm a speech writer for Carmichael," he said.

"I always knew you'd end up working for him."

"Well, not all of us can live in the cities whose streets are paved with gold. I'm surprised you haven't developed an American accent," he teased sarcastically.

Had my accent changed so much? Was it that obvious after all these years of trying out different accents to make a sale over the phone? I could go from California valley-speak through Texas drawl to Brooklynese in no time flat, but I didn't know what I sounded like now.

"You know I don't do accents as well as Damien did."

That was stupid. Trying so hard to hide the details of my life, I'd blundered. Larry and Damien had been lovers since third form, and they had been my only friends at Jamaica College until Reuben came. When Damien had died from AIDS, Larry managed to get my mother's phone number and told her about his funeral. Despite her disapproval, she gave me the message, but my marriage was unraveling and I wasn't good for anyone, let alone Larry. I thought I'd gotten over it until I saw him. I should have come back for Damien's funeral.

There had been many nights in the dorms, after the lights were supposed to be out, that Damien kept us up with his jokes and impressions of the teachers we hated, those whom we'd given nicknames that stuck: Mr. DaCosta, our history teacher, was called "Lenin" because of his pointy beard; Mrs. Douglas, our Spanish teacher, "Amoebae" because Damien said she didn't have a fixed shape or form; but for Dr. McClaren there'd been many failures, including, "Ace of Spades". But that didn't work, so we reverted to "Doc" – father to all the fatherless boys of Standpipe.

"So are you here to stay or only for the funeral, Stew-rat?" he asked using the other nickname Damien had invented.

Thank God Jamaica College trained us to act always as

28

gentlemen. "I don't know," I said. "I'll have to see how things work out."

Larry smiled, hunched his shoulders and folded his arms across his chest. I knew what was going to happen next.

"It may be long, it may be dark, but Sparks, Sparks, we always make our mark," we chanted and exchanged the secret handshake we had developed in the lower school and to which we'd added over the years as we went from Hardy House to Sparks. We were so involved in our own memories that we hadn't noticed Doc behind us.

"You can bugger off now," said Doc in his clipped Oxbridge accent (he had been a Rhodes scholar) that had become even more deliberate since the last time I saw him. A short pug-nosed man with black piercing eyes, he resembled a pit bull and was as fierce (if he wanted to be) as those mongrels that roamed the streets of Kingston.

It was odd to see him out of his customary pith helmet and khaki uniform, but he was just as severe in his school blazer. During the service, his jaw was clenched shut and the tiny muscles at the side of his head quivered, for pride would not allow him to show the briefest hint of emotion, especially in front of the teachers and former students.

"Take care of yourself," said Larry. "Don't be a stranger. Maybe we can get together and have a few drinks," and he walked away without acknowledging Doc.

"So the prodigal has returned," said Doc, with a motion of his hand, dismissing Larry as if we were still students. "How long are you going to be here, Stewart?"

"I don't know. Immigration has only given me three weeks to stay on the island."

"Oh, I see," he paused. "Well, I really think that it's high time that you to came to pick up your father's plaque. It's been there long enough. Cleaned up a bit, and still damaged, but still there. You must come by and pick it up before you leave."

"I'll pick it up as soon as I get a chance."

"Tomorrow," he said. "You're quite lucky that it's still there."

"I'll make the extra effort, Sir," I said. Sir? Like he was some busha on the plantation, parading in the khaki uniform that he wore when he made his circuit around the school. I hadn't used that word in almost fifteen years. This place was already having a bad influence on me.

"I must be going now," I said and walked away from him. I didn't want to talk any more about that plaque. It had caused so much trouble in my life. I spotted Basil's car almost through the gate.

"Basil, Basil, wait it's me, Jason," I shouted. The van stopped and Basil lowered the window.

"Jason! Jason! It's good to see you, man. It really is, but I have to go. I only came to pay my respects. Your father was a good man. But I have to go now."

"What's the rush?"

"Haven't they told you? Everyone fears that supporters from your father's party might be rioting tonight. There's already talk of gang warfare breaking out in St. Thomas, and people like me need to be off the streets before eight."

"What do you mean 'people like you'?"

"If you can, come by and see me. I'll explain what I mean. You know where I am, where I'll always be. Damn, it's good to see you."

"I'll see you then," I said.

"We'll see," said Basil and he wound up the window.

I turned back into the cemetery, looking across the headstones and faded flowers, and saw Chris waving to me. I cut between the cars and began jogging towards him, but was soon out of breath. Working as a telemarketer had robbed me of too many days and nights. When I first left Jamaica I used to play soccer everyday at a park in Carol City, but after I got married I just stopped playing. I was badly out of shape and was taking a beating for it.

"Ah, Benjamin. Why de I still running from oneself?"

It could only have been one person: Papa Legba. I looked around and saw the old Rastaman leaning against a blighted jacaranda. There was no mistaking his broad face and bushy eyebrows that hid his eyes. He wore, as he always had done, a green tam to hold his long stringy locks, some of which tumbled out over his shoulder and chest and merged with his beard. He was wearing his usual calico robes that were edged with scraps of red, green and gold cloth around the sleeves and collar.

Papa Legba held his staff erect and balanced himself against the tree. His staff looked like a long root with a ball of tendrils that resembled a lion's mane balled up at the head.

"Papa Legba, dread. Long time no see."

I had to readjust and listen carefully to Papa Legba. In his vocabulary words had power and everything was sanctified by I. Vital became I-tal, creation became I-ration, behold became I-hold, desire became I-sire. No me, no you. No objects, no victims existed in his world. I-n-I irated the I-niverse. Father, Son and I-ly I-rit. All of I-ration was one.

"Hail Benjamin, Jah-son. Is a long time I man don't see the I. Still in the belly of the dragon, eh. But the I still don't answer I question, why the I still running..."

"I was trying to get to the other side of the..."

"This side and that side, up and down, left and right," said Papa Legba interrupting me. "The I been away too long inna Babylon, living off her mouth water on the edge of the Cannibal Sea. Babylon confuse the I mind, make you forget all that I and I teach the I. So make I ask the question another way. What the I a do right here?"

"I came to my father's funeral. You don't know that Dada died?"

"The I father liveth," said Papa Legba confidently, "not a swallow fall from the sky without I father know."

"What?"

"Is I must ask you, 'what?' Is I must ask the I what him a do in this valley of dry bones?"

"Papa Legba, as usual, you've totally confused me."

"That good," he said and he laughed, almost as if he was teasing, taunting me.

"I'm glad you still find me amusing, but I have to go now," I said. "I'm sorry, I don't have the time just now for your riddles."

Papa Legba continued to laugh, then stopped abruptly, "The I don't have the time to find the serpent that make de I father pass through to another i-bration?"

I came closer to him. "You know who killed Dada?" I said. "You know who killed him and you haven't gone to the police?"

I knew at once I shouldn't have been so abrupt with him. He was the one who had taken me to a groundation ceremony, days of meditation and drumming, up in the hills of Wareika. He said I would have to find my centre before I went off to live in Babylon. From the looks of it, the ceremony hadn't worked.

"I man don't deal with Babylon," he said. "Plus, Babylon say I man mad, and I nah go mad house again."

"Then tell me," I said, because I knew he would never tell the police. I still remembered the time they took him off to Bellevue because he was standing at Half Way Tree screaming and covering his ears, saying he could hear the stars falling and burning from the heavens. Another time, he said he was going to complain to the Governor General to tell Queen Elizabeth to stop the war against the children of Israel. That time Dada got him out of Bellevue.

"More time," he said as he looked over my shoulder. "Them a call de I. I man will see the I later, but not here. It grieve I soul to be around these stone."

"Okay," I said, "but where are you going?"

"First, everywhere and then nowhere," he said. "Trust oneself and I and I will lead the way."

"See," I said, "more riddles!"

"Riggles," said Papa Legba, "the I think I man is a spider man?"

"I'm not too sure."

Papa Legba shook his head and waved goodbye to me. I walked away from him and went towards the car where Chris was waiting for me.

"Who were you talking with over there?"

"Papa Legba," I said.

"Papa Legba? I heard he was dead. So what does he have to say for himself?"

"He says he knows who killed Dada."

"Did he say who?"

"Yes." I couldn't resist the temptation, for Chris had always said he didn't have the time for Rasta nonsense. "He said a serpent killed him."

"Then, for once I agree with him," said Chris.

"What?"

"Yeah, and that snake is Carmichael. But c'mon get in the car."

Chris motioned to the family bodyguards, Cedrick and Trini, and they got in the back with him. The driver, Tony, was the son of a former maid of the family. He was wearing dark glasses and a New York Yankees cap, so I couldn't tell if he was still scowling at me the way he used to when we were growing up. For some reason, he hated me then and he didn't seem exactly friendly now.

As the car went through the gates, I could see Papa Legba limping through the open land beside the cemetery. He was surrounded by several mongrels that were jumping up and down and around his staff. He waved to me and I rolled down the window and waved back.

The car veered away from the boulevard that led to Standpipe, Carmichael's constituency. All the stores above Matilda's corner were deserted and security lights outside a pharmacy flickered in silence. The stores had been battened down and metal awnings and hurricane shutters were in place. Soldiers were rolling bundles of barbed wire across the streets. Nothing was coming in and out of Mona Heights and Hope Pastures, except local traffic through the back roads. Standpipe was shut down.

As we passed through a mass of JLP supporters, Chris looked up from some notes he was studying and waved, flashing the victory sign to a group of boys who were running beside the car. They cheered Chris and unfurled a sheet spray-painted in red, *Death to the murderer, Carmichael.*

"That's one crazy Rastaman," said Tony, trying to start a conversation.

"Yeah," I said, "real crazy."

CHAPTER THREE

Shifting to a lower gear, Tony eased the strain on the engine. The car groaned up Beverly Hills with the load of party leaflets that Chris had crammed into the trunk that was already filled with brochures from Anastasia's, the guest-house on the north coast that he owned.

Anastasia's had begun as a small art gallery, Savacou, that Emma had run until she retired and became a housewife. Chris, with only a minimal loan from Dada, had built the hotel around the art gallery, and as far as I could tell was doing well. He chose the name, Anastasia's, because he was always interested in Russian literature and had flirted with becoming a full professor at a small college in California. But after failing to gain tenure (they claimed his publications credits weren't prestigious; he claimed racism) he wandered around the West Coast before he came back to the island. "Better to be a big fish in a small pond," he wrote in his last letter before I stopped writing to him. Since then, he'd been trying his hand at everything until he finally settled down as an hotelier.

As we came around the corner that led to the dead-end street where we lived, I noticed immediately the change in the neighbourhood. It was a hodgepodge of architectural designs whose only purpose was to announce wealth and bad taste. Several of the new homes resembled homes in Miami that had replicated themselves exponentially across the state: a *faux* Mediterranean style that reduced the form to stucco, arches, and red tile, instead of a breezy openness that celebrated, yet resisted, the sun, wind, and rain.

I could see the outline of the silkcotton tree that grew in the canal behind our house. Its branches spread out and seemed to net mockingbirds and parrots that flew across the twilight sky. Its shadow fell across the banks of the stream that coursed through the canal and at one time provided water for the area.

At the entrance to the street, a soldier and a policeman stopped the car, checked our ID and allowed us to pass through the barricade. Our house, a two-story colonial, retreated into the landscape with its strategically placed palms and banyans, with splashes of the red ginger's fire near the corners.

Our street had been cordoned off and only residents and the press had been allowed to enter. Sharpshooters peered over the tops of the roofs and soldiers hid behind the bushes. The reason soon became clear. Carmichael's car was parked on the drive.

"That fucker," said Chris. "What's he trying to do, show me up in my own house?"

"Take it easy," I said, "he's probably here to talk with Emma. They were always good friends."

"Good friends don't count these days," he said. But that was Chris. He scrutinized everyone's actions and found selfish motives behind the most innocent gesture. Before the car could come to a stop, Cedrick flicked open the door and he and Trini jumped out of the car.

Flashbulbs exploded. The verandah was filled with a bevy of reporters with thick yellow pads and miniature tape recorders who surged towards Chris as he tried to enter the house.

"Mr. Lumley, Mr. Lumley, although you were passed over by your father for a ministerial position, are you planning to run for your father's seat in the upcoming election?" asked the reporter from *The Gleaner*.

36

Chris eased over to the threshold of the door and waited for Cedrick and Trini to put themselves between him and the reporters.

"Albert Lumley," he said, "was a true hero. In a time when all our heroes are dead, my father was a hero for our nation. But now he is gone. But he had one goal that can never be killed or extinguished. He wanted to see one Jamaica. A Jamaica, not for the rich and the poor, not for the high and the low, but one people united under the ideals of democracy. But the tragedy is that he was murdered by the enemies of democracy."

"So who are these murderers of democracy?" asked the reporter from *The Star*. "What about the rumours that his death was a direct hit by a Standpipe posse? Has his gun or any other personal belongings been recovered?"

"We will let the police and the courts decide that," said Chris, "because that's what my father would have wanted. He was a man of whom it could be said, he lived not only the letter of the law, but also its spirit."

"You still haven't answered the question about the election," shouted the reporter from *The Gleaner*.

"I am mourning the death of my father," said Chris, his voice breaking with emotion. "Please allow me the chance to pause and to mourn. But this much I will say. If I were to run, I would want to create a Jamaica in which there is honesty with one's friends, courage against one's enemies, generosity for the weak, and courtesy, respect at all times. If we keep these thoughts before us, we will never fear the future of our island, and all the brave heroes who have passed before my father. Marcus Garvey, Sam Sharpe, Paul Bogle will not have died in vain." He slipped through the door as Cedrick and Trini barred the reporters from entering the house.

I made my way past the privet hedge and around the house, through the narrow passage between the kitchen and the maid's quarters. When I got inside the living room Chris was pacing around, while Carmichael and Emma were sitting on the sofa having a cup of coffee.

"Hello, Emma, Uncle David," I said, looking around the room. "Where's Nicole?"

"She was so tired. She's upstairs in the guest room taking a nap," said Emma. "Would you like some coffee, Jason?"

"No thanks," I said. "I don't drink that Babylon tea any more. I have a hard enough time falling asleep at night."

Emma, by contrast, could drink coffee at any time of the day without it affecting her. She was a caffeine addict. Always the first to wake up, she'd stumble to the kitchen and brew herself a pot of coffee that she would finish before we'd started our first cup.

I moved closer to them, carefully avoiding the weights of the cuckoo clock Dada had bought for Emma when he went to Switzerland for an International Law of the Sea Conference in Berne. An early painting by Karl Parboosingh hung on the right of the clock and across to the left was an iron sculpture by one of Emma's favourite Haitian artists, Georges Litaud.

Emma seemed sadder than at the funeral, and she held Carmichael's hand tightly. Could he really have had Dada killed and be sitting in his living room holding his widow's hand?

"So, Chris," said Emma, "aren't you going to say hello to your Uncle David?"

Chris mumbled a greeting under his breath and walked over to Dada's armchair. He turned the chair away from the sofa and pointed it towards the window. Outside, Trini was handing out the leaflets to the reporters.

"I think I better be going now," said Carmichael, and kissed Emma on her cheek. "If you need anything, call me."

"Our father," said Chris contemptuously, "provided everything for us when he died. We don't need charity."

"Charity," replied Carmichael, "was never my intention."

Chris pulled down the footrest and stretched out, thrumming his fingers on the side of the chair. Chris had never liked Carmichael, and his hatred increased when Carmichael gave a speech about ostentation and the growing American influence on the youth. Chris had just come back from the States in the late seventies wearing his Italian suits, silk shirts, and Brooks Brothers loafers, and although Carmichael didn't use Chris' name, everyone knew who he was talking about. Chris could have killed him.

"You're right, Uncle David," he said sarcastically and glared at me. "No one could ever accuse you of ulterior motives."

Carmichael was about to answer him when Emma stood up and grabbed him by the arm. She held out her hand inviting me to accompany them. As we walked to the door, she straightened the flower in the lapel of his jacket.

"David, you've always been one of my dearest friends. Of course, I'll call," she said.

Chris glared at her. According to Chris, Emma had cost Dada his chance to become the Prime Minister. She was several shades lighter than my mother and Dada hadn't had the good sense to keep Emma in the background until after the elections were over. With the scandal that surrounded his marriage to Emma, he forfeited his chance for political immortality and almost lost his seat in parliament, but Dada didn't seem to mind.

"Take care of yourself. Eat. And get some sleep," Carmichael said playfully. "You haven't looked this bad since that party up in Irish Town when you had that awful hangover," and he gave her a hug before he opened the door.

"Jason, walk with me, nuh," he said, turning on the charm. "We haven't talked in a long time."

I was always amazed at how he did this. He could go from the most mundane topic and with just a slight flutter in the timbre of his voice he'd win over his audience, no matter how opposed they had been to him. All the things I'd learned in sales manuals – making and kept eye contact – he had perfected by following his intuition and keen intelligence.

As we walked down the driveway, a photographer lurking in the bushes took our pictures and scurried out of sight. Carmichael's driver, Victor, opened the door and Jagga brought him the flyer that Trini had been giving to the reporters.

"Look at this," said Carmichael. "This is the type of irresponsibility that I've been trying to stop all week."

I took the flyer from him and glanced over the cartoon of Carmichael and Dada. The cartoon had three frames. In the first frame there was a pile of dead bodies over which Carmichael presided. Underneath the pile was a caption "Tribal War". In the second frame was a caricature of Dada in a bloodied Roman toga. Carmichael was behind him and held a bloody knife over his head. In the third frame Dada was on top of the pile and there was a caption: "*Et tu*, Carmichael?"

As I looked at the cartoon, the question burned on my tongue and I felt like blurting out, "Did you kill Dada?" But I held back, I respected him too much to ask. But everything so far convinced me that only someone as powerful as Carmichael could have had Dada killed.

I glanced over the cartoon again and I tried not to show my amusement, but when Carmichael looked at me sternly I couldn't help myself.

"I must admit it's pretty funny."

"It's almost criminal," he said, then softened his tone. "But I wouldn't expect you to understand this. Things have changed since you left."

"I know, everyone keeps telling me."

"It could change for the better if people like you stayed here," he said, "but I suspect you're going to be leaving soon."

"I'll be leaving on Sunday," I said, trying to sound as if I really knew what I was talking about.

"That's too bad, too bad," he said. "I wish you were staying. I'm sure that's what your father would have wanted."

I was surprised when he said this. It was the first time that I heard him speak so tenderly about Dada. Rivals in love for Emma, they had once been friends, but since the country's independence they had also become political enemies. When

Dada divorced my mother and married Emma, Carmichael further distanced himself and only spoke to Dada over the parliament floor in the manner reserved for debates, "As the esteemed Minister of Justice well knows..."

"I'd like to come back," I said, "but every time I think about it, something bad happens. So I've stayed away."

"That's no excuse," he said. "Bad things happen everywhere. Don't let your love for the island stop you from coming back."

"My love?"

"Yes, your love," he said. "You love this place as much as I do and this is why I wish you could stay. The country needs young people like you."

Like me, I thought. More telemarketers?

"I have nothing against Chris. He's your father's son. Your father and I were the old guard, we saw the birth of the country. We need your help so it can keep growing in the right direction. We need your help, Jason."

"My help? How can I help?"

"To begin, with," he said, "you can help me by talking to your brother. He shouldn't be wasting his talents on propaganda like this. He should be building up the country, not tearing it down."

Even though I knew he was setting me up, I nodded with him, then looked down at the pavement. Stubborn weeds that had resisted Dada and a whole army of gardeners' efforts pushed through the concrete, spilling their seeds into the cracks.

"Chris has never listened to anyone before, so why should he listen to me now?"

"I know. He never listened to his father or Emma, but maybe he'll listen to you, now that he's older and gotten over his jealousy of you."

"Why should he be jealous of me? He's the one with the brains, the looks, the talent."

"From what Emma told me, he always felt he was in competition with you for Albert's affection."

41

"He can have it," I said. "I was never in any competition for it with him. He was always the one who made Emma and me feel like outsiders."

"Well, think of this as an opportunity to rejoin your family, to rejoin the life of your country."

He made it sound as if I was dead. Maybe I was. In Miami, race and nationality kept me out of the mainstream – and hanging out in Churchill's wasn't helping.

"Give it a try," said Carmichael. "Appeal to Chris in the name of tradition or something like that. I know how you Jamaica College Old Boys think, how you value tradition and service to others. And you, Jason, are the quintessential Jamaica College Old Boy."

"Okay, I'll talk with him," I said, ignoring the insult, his allusion to a time of high ideals, pomp, and colonialism. "But I won't make any promises."

"Don't worry," said Carmichael. "Your father made too many promises that he couldn't keep. Why pass that on to the next generation?"

Carmichael strolled over to his car and his bodyguards ran over to his side and got in with him. The car rolled out of the driveway and a police car sped ahead of them. Soldiers who had been in hiding around the neighbourhood piled into the truck that had been parked at the end of the road, and the motorcade slowly made its way down the hill.

As I watched the last reporters leave, Chris came outside and stood in front of one of the crotons. He tore off a twig and squeezed the leaves between his fingers. I folded the flyer and put it my pocket.

"What were you two talking about?" he asked.

"Nothing," I said.

"Nothing! Carmichael never talks about nothing. What did he want?"

"If you must know," I said, "he has high hopes for you."

"I bet he has," sneered Chris. "I bet he has."

I ignored him and went inside to the living room. Emma was stretched out on the sofa and looked as if she was about to fall asleep. When she saw me, she stood up, composed herself, wrapping her veil around her neck.

"Boys, I'm going upstairs to get some sleep. I'll say my goodnight now. Jason, the maids have fixed up your old room. And I've had them prepare a special meal for you, your favourite, ox tail."

"It will be a great improvement on what passes as Jamaican food in Miami."

"You can only get the real thing here, Jason. Only here."

"Thank you, Emma," I said, and sat down at the dining room table.

She hurried up the stairs, then turned and said, "Good night, Chris. Take care of Jason. Oh, and could you replace the security lights outside. I think the left one is blown."

Chris ignored her. He went into the kitchen and began cutting some hardo bread and putting a piece of chicken in the microwave. Emma came back down the stairs.

"Is something bothering you, Chris? I thought I said goodnight."

"Goodnight, Emma," he said reluctantly. The microwave beeped and Chris took out the chicken.

Emma turned and went back up the stairs. She was almost at the top when Chris came out of the kitchen.

"As a matter of fact, Emma," he said, looking up at her, "there is something wrong. Something is bothering me."

Emma paused, her hands grasping the railing. "And what exactly is bothering you?"

"You know, Emma. You know."

Chris turned away from her and went to sit down in the living room to eat. He was breaking off a tiny piece of bread when Emma came down the stairs again and stood in front of him.

"What do I know, Christopher?"

"You know, Emma," he said. "You know."

"What are you talking about?"

"Okay, Emma, I'll tell you since you pretend you don't know. How could you carry on like that with Carmichael at the funeral."

Emma was flustered. "First of all," she said, "I was not carrying on with anyone at the funeral. And if I was carrying on with anyone, David Carmichael included, it would be none of your business!"

"For God's sake, my father was barely in the ground."

"David Carmichael is one of my dearest friends. We were friends before you were born. I don't care what you say about him on the streets, that's politics. That's none of my business. But I won't have it here, not in my house. Your father respected my wishes and he never discussed politics, except in his den, and I expect you to do the same. Do you understand me?"

"Yes, Emma," he said.

She pulled the veil from around her neck and tried to cover her eyes, but the tears were already streaming down her face.

"The least you could have done," he said, "was not to hold Carmichael's hands in front of the press. It wasn't good for your already tattered reputation and it wasn't good for the party to have Albert Lumley's widow holding hands with the leader of the opposition. The last thing this family needs is a sexual scandal in the papers."

"I will hold anyone's hand that it pleases me to hold. You have no right to criticize anything that I do. And as for your precious party, I don't care what happens. It has already wrecked too many lives, too many families, and too many friendships. Now, leave me alone. I refuse to be involved any more!"

She turned and made her way up the stairs to her bedroom at the end of the hallway. She closed the door behind her, but I could hear her sobbing.

These two had been fighting for as long as I'd known them. Without Dada, they would be going at each other without restraint. And Chris would win. I got up and went into the kitchen for a beer. I wasn't thirsty, but I needed to hold something. I'd always avoided getting involved in their petty disputes – none of my business – but this time I had to say something. Emma had brought us up and we owed her some respect – though this was not always how I'd felt.

When, on one of my vacation trips to Miami, my mother told me what had happened between her, my father and Emma, I hated Emma. But then my mother said that Dada was the one to blame; he was the snake in the grass who went out of his way to seduce two first cousins who had grown up together like sisters. If my mother had forgiven Emma, so must I.

"Chris, what's wrong with you?" I asked. "She was already upset. What did you have to do that for?"

Chris chewed on a gristly bit of chicken, then delicately removed a tiny bone with his finger. He looked at it disdainfully, almost as if he was ashamed of his own hunger.

"Jason, Jason," he said condescendingly, "you're so forgiving. She's not going to handicap another election. The papers will have a scandal tomorrow if I don't call in a few favours. Believe me she needs all the help she can get."

"So you'd be doing it for her?"

"Of course, I would," he said. "Technically, she *is* our mother – and, of course, though we're leading in the polls, this could cost us a few points that we can't afford."

"Or you could gain a few," I said.

"What do you know? Emma's like every woman in Jamaica that I know, only wants to lie down with a man if she can collect his money after he's dead."

"That's not exactly fair."

"After your divorce, I would have thought you'd agree with me."

"My divorce has nothing to do with how you're treating Emma."

"Doesn't it?" he said snidely. "Think about how Dada treated your mother. My mother died waiting to get a penny from him. So I'll be damned if Emma gets any of his money."

Chris walked away from me into the kitchen, wiped his finger with the napkin and emptied the gristle into the wastebasket. He still had the same deliberate intensity. That was when I realized what he was up to.

"You're going to run, aren't you?"

Why Chris would run for political office baffled me. He'd never shown any inkling towards politics for as long as I'd known him. I hoped it wasn't merely for the power he would wield. We'd had too many politicians like that. The kind who'd sold us out over Federation, bauxite deals, and free trade zones – and then had the nerve to get up on a soapbox and rail about colonialism and slavery.

"There's no one better qualified to take over the work that Albert left behind."

"Doesn't that take a lot of money?"

"I have enough," he said. "The guest house is doing fine. Don't worry, by the time all of this is over I'll have enough," and he went down to the garage.

I went to the kitchen, found a Red Stripe in the back of the fridge, opened it, and plopped down on the sofa. My shoes were filthy. Mud had hardened inside the crease and the laces were soiled. I took off my shoes and socks and put my feet on the wooden floor and felt the moist coldness. I was home.

I took the flyer out of my pocket and looked at it again. As I was about to ball it up and throw it away, Chris walked back into the living room. He was carrying his gun-cleaning kit, two old T-shirts, and his revolver. He zipped open the holster and laid out a T-shirt over the coffee table. He put another T-shirt on the floor.

"You planning on using that?" I asked.

"I'm going down to the country, to the hotel," he said and brought a chair from the dining room. He sat down and flicked the thumb latch of the gun and removed the bullets from the cylinder. "So do you like my artwork?"

"It's all you," I said.

"I knew you'd like it," he said. "It's very theatrical and Jamaicans love drama in their politics. It should go over well."

"I didn't say I liked it. I said it was all you – peddling insinuation as fact."

"What do you mean?"

"You really don't think Uncle David killed Dada, do you?"

"For God's sake, Jason, stop calling him Uncle David."

"It's a habit. You used to call him..."

"Yeah, but call him anything but uncle. Call him what you used to call Dada under your breath, that son-of-a-bitch!"

Chris chuckled to himself. He re-checked the cylinder and assembled the cleaning rod. It didn't make sense to me. Carmichael had been one of the richest men in the island and was proud of saying how he had built himself up from nothing with his poultry farms – unlike our family that had inherited our wealth over generations.

"But besides politics, why would he want to kill Dada?"

"Besides politics?" said Chris. "It's the only game in town."

"As I said, besides politics, why would Carmichael kill Dada?"

"Why does anyone kill someone?"

"I don't know."

"For money, for power. Didn't you see all those Old Boys with their fancy cars and expensive wives? Jamaican women are very expensive. They demand a first world lifestyle in a Third World country. We could pay off the entire national debt with all the Saabs, Porches, Volvos, and BMW's that were in the parking lot."

"Why would he kill Dada for money? With his poultry business he should be a millionaire several times over."

"Should have been," said Chris slyly, wiping the barrel with the "Magic" cloth that came with the cleaning kit. "But socialists make bad business men. He wasn't insured and when hurricane Gilbert passed through, it wiped him out, and he didn't have the government's money to rebuild at the taxpayers' expense. The next year, when he thought he was going to be back on his feet, a strange virus killed off most of his chickens. He claims it was a CIA plot because only his chickens were affected. Now he's practically penniless. He may even owe some people money."

"That doesn't sound like the David Carmichael I used to know. How do you know this is true?"

"From our father," he said. He eased the steel brush into the barrel and twisted the handle of the cleaning rod. After the rod had been fed about three inches, he grasped the handle and pushed the rod straight in, careful not to nick the inside or edges.

"He knew everything. All those brilliant speeches, accurate predictions, he was getting help from everywhere. Washington, London. When Carmichael was in power, right under his very nose in the Ministry of Finance, people were pulling files and giving them to our father."

"So how does all this tie in?"

"Dada called in all his favours and, single-handedly, introduced a bill to make any business that had criminal connections, similar to RICO in America, subject to government confiscation. Carmichael went into business with some of his ministers, probably without knowing what they were really doing – I'll give him that much – but they were caught shipping cocaine. Carmichael stood to lose everything because you know, with our father, if it was illegal, he would prosecute to the fullest extent of the law. No matter who was involved."

"But are you certain Carmichael was involved?"

"Didn't you see that woman who attacked him today! Everybody knows it's Carmichael. Now we have to find the proof. The guy who Dada killed was from Standpipe, and Carmichael controls Standpipe. All the evidence points in his direction. He's the only one who could have authorized it. As Dada used to say, sometimes in politics you don't have to prove anything, you only have to point."

Chris removed the rod and cleaned the barrel and handle with the "Magic" cloth. He fitted a patch saturated with cleaning solution on the rod and pushed it through the bore and out the muzzle, pointing it towards the coffee table so the loosened particles would fall on the T-shirt. When he was sure most of the fouling was removed, he put on another saturated patch.

"So how come Dada was the only one killed? Where were the body guards?"

"Lone wolf Lumley," said Chris disdainfully, and put a dry patch on the rod. "Whenever he felt he was on to something important, he always did it alone so he always had all the glory, so all the spotlight would be on him. He was always leaving in the middle of the night to follow some lead..."

"Or some woman's skirt," I added.

"That's another story," he said and put on another dry patch. Chris, unlike me, never took Dada's infidelities seriously. He saw it as part of living in Jamaica, and for a politician not to have a mistress was a liability. I didn't know what Chris was up to in this respect, for although he had been associated with several women, including a few Miss Jamaica contestants, he had never been seriously involved with any one woman. He was still unattached, and I think that was how he wanted it. He had already proven himself and his prowess, so there was no need to keep up the game.

"He went alone that night and that's how he was killed. That's what the police on our side are saying."

He stressed the words *our side*. The police were known to suppress or discover evidence depending on how rich you were or your political affiliation. Depending on where you were arrested, saying a single name could mean life or death.

"So what about the missing papers that the news people were making so much fuss about? Why are you saying something different to the press?"

"Hype. The newspapers trying to sell more copies," he said wearily. "The police on our side say there's nothing to it. And I have to score my own points against Carmichael. You know we Jamaicans need conspiracies to feed our imaginations. Like the rumour the CIA killed Bob Marley. Excitement, drama. I'm kind of tired of it myself."

"So what are you going to do now?"

"Me?" said Chris, "I'm going upstairs to take a shower. They'll soon be locking off the water. There's a drought on you know." He rubbed the bore, using about four more patches, until he felt it was dry.

"The usual summer lock-offs?"

"The same," he said. "Goodnight, Jason."

He gathered up the dirty patches in the T-shirt, dabbed some oil around the cylinder and hammer and wiped away the excess. He put the cylinder back in place and reloaded the gun. Before he closed it in the holster, he cleaned the hammer with a nylon toothbrush and wiped the handle.

Chris cleaned his fingers with alcohol wipes he had in his pocket, patted me on the shoulder, picked up his things and went upstairs to his room. I slumped back on the sofa and gazed around the room.

"Goodnight Chris," I said.

I pulled off my tie and unbuttoned my shirt. I thought I'd relax a bit before going up to see Nicole. I closed my eyes to see if I could still hear the sound of the stream behind the house. All I could hear were the wheels whirring inside the clock on the wall.

I opened my eyes and looked over to my father's office. Since I'd come back, things that at first had seemed alien were becoming familiar again. What had been out of place, now had a certain rightness. I remembered once walking on the marl roads of the small town where my mother had been born and she had often talked about. Now, again, I felt like an explorer in known territory.

I wandered inside the office and over to the library where I would sneak, whenever Dada was away, to read his books. I used to curl up on his chaise longue with novels by George Lamming, V. S. Naipaul and John Hearne. Surrounded by oak panels, paintings by Barrington Watson and Cecil Baugh, the musty old law books with their gilt edges fading, and the almost antiseptic smell of the newer books, I lost myself in that room.

I'd been studying for my GCE O levels and Dada had come home earlier than I expected. He rubbed my forehead and I jumped up from the chaise longue where I'd been dozing. A copy of C.L.R James' *The Black Jacobins* fell off my chest and onto the floor. Dada picked up the book and gave it back to me. I covered the front of the book when it was back in my hands.

"Why are you hiding it?" he asked. "You think I would be ashamed of you or that I don't know what's inside that book?"

"You've read C.L.R. James?" I asked in disbelief. Dada could never have been thought of as a radical.

"And Franz Fanon, Eldridge Cleaver, and Walter Rodney. In fact, I've read all of the books that the Prime Minister has banned." He must have been lying.

"So why have you gone along with Doc and the others?"

"Who says I've gone along with them? I don't think any books should be banned."

"So you're enforcing a law that's basically immoral. You should either oppose it or resign," I said contemptuously.

"I prefer to turn a blind eye. The Prime Minister is better served by my dissent behind closed doors, than if I am replaced by a sycophant."

He went over to his desk and opened the bottom drawer. He took out a brand new copy of Tony McNeill's *Reel From the Life-Movie* and threw it on my lap.

"I noticed you were reading Wordsworth for your O levels. Here, read McNeill. He has a great line: 'This morning I chose to stay home, to watch the cats and think of Columbus. And the grass is precious merely because it belongs to us.'"

I was impressed. He actually knew the lines by heart. But then again he was a lawyer.

"But I'm interested in where you got that James book. Don't worry, I won't go raiding their libraries."

"Basil Cunningham gave it to me," I said reluctantly.

"I figured as much," he said and scratched his head. "Interesting painter, misguided, but interesting."

Misguided? How? How dare he attack Basil when Basil took more time with me to explain everything that was happening in the island? Or was he just hinting at the rumour that Basil was a homosexual?

"What do you mean by misguided?" I asked.

"It isn't for the reasons you're thinking," he said sternly. "Basil Cunningham has unfortunately bought into the whole socialist claptrap about the redistribution of wealth. Redistributing wealth only makes all of us poorer. It goes against everything in nature that seeks abundance. It doesn't help the poor in the least."

"It gives them food," I countered.

"It's better to teach a man to fish than..."

"To give him a fish every day." I finished his sentence. "But how can you just sit there and watch the suffering all around you."

"Who says I'm sitting around doing nothing. I'm doing all I can with what I have. All I can do is to give all I have, and hope others will do the same. I hope you'll do the same. And as for Basil Cunningham, if he thinks we're awful by banning these books, tell him to go to Cuba and speak his mind."

"What happens in Cuba has nothing to do with what's happening in Jamaica."

"That's precisely my point," he said. "What's happening in Jamaica is like nothing that's happening anywhere else. You should read James more carefully. He says the Caribbean is an 'original pattern, not European, not African, not a part of the American main, but *sui generis,* with no parallel anywhere else'. I'll lend you my copy of *From Toussaint L'Ouverture to Fidel Castro* when you're older. We can talk about it some time."

We never did.

★★★

The mahogany desk shone with the light from the living room. I sat in the leather chair and turned on the lamp and saw my face gazing back at me. It was in a group of photos, and was the only picture from my adolescence in which I was smiling. I'd gone bird shooting down in Westmoreland with Dada and Chris. I'd shot my first duck. Dada had taught us from an early age how to handle and clean guns, and Emma was a pretty good shot herself. But they had always given us stern warnings about never pointing the gun at anyone except in self-defence. I was smiling in the picture because Chris had been whispering in my ear, "We could shoot him right now. We could get away with it. We could say it was an accident, everyone would believe us." I was laughing so hard, I thought I was going to be sick. Dada snapped the picture and now it was on his desk.

I got up and walked around the room and was examining a first edition of George Campbell's *First Poems* and a battered copy of *In a Green Night* when the phone rang.

"Lumley residence," I said.

"Benjamin?"

"Who is this?"

"Is Reuben. Reuben, your brethren."

Reuben, my brethren. My idren from the days of Papa Legba and the Rasta camp. Reuben, my idren with whom I spent a whole night with the elders chanting down Babylon until the early morning light.

I picked up one of Dada's pens and began doodling one of my favourite designs on a legal pad: a palm tree, the sun and the shadow of the palm on the sand. I added some squares and circles to the design. When I had first come to America, several of my art teachers in college had convinced me I was a good draughtsman, but I would never be an artist. I began doodling. I did the things that I knew I could do without the fear of failure.

"Reuben! I thought you were in England playing pro soccer, or at least be playing for the Reggae Boyz."

"Things never work out," he said. "Knee injury."

"So what's up? How come you're calling me here?"

"That's what I call to ask you," he said. "I see you on television today."

"My father's funeral." I was tired and I didn't want to go through long discussion over the phone. I had completely encircled the palm tree with squares and circles.

"Raas," he said, "raas, raas, raas, raas."

"What's wrong?" I said. "What's wrong?"

"Nothing, nothing at all. So how you doing, my striker? I bet all that American food get you so fat you can't play ball no more."

My striker. I hadn't been called that in fifteen years. Reuben, my linkman, my mid-field general who could find me anywhere. I could still hear his voice urging me on for the last time we went on a five mile jog up Jack's Hill and I was about to give up and he called to me, "Benjamin, just one more corner and we'll make it." And he grabbed my arm and together we made it around the bend where we could see the coach, standing by his car, talking with one of the underage girls on her way up the hill and ignoring us. Without Reuben I never would have finished that race. Without Reuben I never would have had that moment of exhilaration that has stayed with me to this day – that moment, that feeling of success that I had now traded for failure.

"Benjamin," he said, "I need to see you. Me in trouble."

"What kind of trouble?"

"I cyaan tell you now, but I haffi see you. But you can't tell a soul, not a soul."

I tried to make a path from the bottom of the page to the centre of the drawing, but ended up in a dead end of squares.

"What's the big secret?"

"I will tell you when I see you," he said. "One thing though. Why you never tell me Albert Lumley was your father?"

I wasn't going to go through the whole long story with him, so I played along.

"You never asked."

"You right," he said. "You right to raas. I gone now. See you tomorrow at about twelve o'clock at Hardy House. You remember where that is?"

He chuckled.

"Yeah, I remember. I'll see you then."

I hung up the phone and Chris came inside the office. He had finished showering and was in his pajamas.

"You still up?" he asked.

"Yeah, but I was going upstairs to get some sleep, big day tomorrow."

"Big day? How come I don't know about this?"

"I'm meeting one of my friends from JC. Old friend from my soccer days." I needed to win Chris' confidence in case I really needed his help in the future, so I told him.

"You mean the Rasta days. So do I know this old friend?"

"No. You were still studying in California."

"So where are you meeting him? I'll have Tony drive you."

"Jamaica College."

"Jamaica College! You can't go there."

I had traced the line into another dead end. This time I would try from outside the margin.

"Why?"

"Jamaica College is now a part of Standpipe. Carmichael gerrymandered it into his constituency the last time he was in power. His offices were firebombed so everything above Matilda's corner is off limits to outsiders. They don't trust anyone. You'd have to go through the soldiers and police and then Carmichael's people to get through Standpipe. You can't go there."

"I have to."

"Why?"

"It's personal. He was the only real friend I had at Jamaica College."

I wasn't going to tell the whole truth, all he needed to know was he was my Rasta idren.

"What was his name again?" Chris asked.

"Reuben," I said just to annoy him, again.

"I mean his real name," said Chris.

I was about to say that Reuben was his real name when I saw from the expression on Chris's face that he was becoming impatient. Getting Chris to listen to anything vaguely connected with Rasta was like trying to get a Mormon to appreciate the subtleties of Family Man's melodic bass line. At first I couldn't remember Reuben's Christian name, but then it came to me.

"Adrian," I said, "Adrian Matthews."

Finally the centre. I extended the rays of the sun to resemble a Rastaman's dreadlocks. The dreadlocks merged with the palm fronds and the shadows.

"Doesn't ring a bell."

"I told you," I said, "he was well after your time at Jamaica College."

"Either way you're not going," said Chris.

"I don't remember asking your permission."

Chris knew it was no use arguing. He couldn't stop me because once I'd made up my mind, I was rarely deterred. This involved Reuben; I was not going to be stopped.

He went into the kitchen, jumped up on the counter and opened a cupboard, searching in it until he found a box of floodlights. He jumped down and pulled one of the lights out of the box.

"Although it would do wonders for my campaign to have a second Lumley killed in the space of one week, and killed in Standpipe at that, my career is not worth your life, Jason. You can't go."

"Why can't I go?"

"Standpipe is too dangerous for you. You'd be dead before you crossed the boulevard."

"I'll call Carmichael," I said defiantly. "He'll help me." And he heard the determination in my voice.

"What's so important about him that you'd risk your life?"

I ignored him.

Chris walked over to the light switch and flicked it three times. Cedrick came up to the door and Chris turned the dead bolt. He handed the floodlight to Cedrick and closed the door.

"If we figure out a way to get you into Standpipe," said Chris, "Tony has to go with you for protection."

"I don't need protection."

"Dada said the same thing and now he's cold. Besides, I don't trust anyone from Standpipe."

"But why would anyone want to hurt me? I'm nobody," I said. "And besides, he's my friend." I said.

"Yeah, right," said Chris.

CHAPTER FOUR

Nicole's room faced an open stretch of land that, over the years, had come to be known as Legba's Claim. The police and the courts under Carmichael had tried to evict Papa Legba several times, but Dada had defended him and Papa Legba kept the land. When I left the island the case had still not been settled.

I knocked on the door and it swung open. Nicole's bed was empty and the screen door to the balcony was ajar. I knocked again.

"I'm out on the balcony."

She'd found one of the lawn chairs that Emma kept in the closet and was enjoying the breeze that swept down from Wareika and through the valley of the Hope River.

"This is wonderful." Nicole had removed her make-up and had changed into a yellow cotton dress that reflected the last rays of the setting sun in the pleats and hollows around her waist. Her green eyes had a far away look. She had been staring into the horizon, rocking her heels against the edge of the balcony.

"So this is where you grew up. I finally get to see the place," she said and lowered her feet to rest against the bottom of the railing. Her skirt parted across her thighs.

"Coming back to Jamaica was the best thing I ever did. Everything feels so familiar. I know this sounds weird, but there is something here that makes me feel so close to everything, like I belong here, like a part of me never left here."

Although she was born in Jamaica, this was her first time in Kingston. She'd grown up in Mandeville and her father had left for the States when she was twelve years old. Since then she'd lived in Miami where I'd met her.

She pointed to a mound. "Don't tell me, don't tell me, that's where your brother used to play King of the Hill."

"How did you remember that?"

"But what's that over there?" she asked.

"Those are the foundations of the Great House my great grandfather built. It was burned down in a mysterious fire. This house is built where the barracks used to be. All of this sprang from the mind of my great grandfather and he put in every brick all by himself."

"Probably with the help of a few slaves."

"Yeah, it's not something that I'm proud of, but it's a historical fact. Like the Morant Bay Rebellion occurred in 1865. That's all."

"Maybe to you," she said as her eyes swept the landscape. I let it pass. I wasn't going to get into a discussion about family trees with Nicole, because everyone in Jamaica has someone white, someone black, someone East Indian and someone Chinese somewhere in their family. Besides, her great-grandfather was Dutch.

"And that tree, it's so huge."

"That's the famous silkcotton tree that's supposed to be haunted."

"Says who?"

"Papa Legba, the old Rastaman. I saw him today. And get this. He claims that my father's death wasn't a robbery as the police say, but that it was a deliberate murder. Chris, the last person on earth I would ever expect to agree with Papa Legba, thinks David Carmichael was behind it."

"The man who was with Emma? No. You're just saying that to scare me," she said.

I came closer to her and began toying with the buttons on her dress.

"I don't believe it myself. He and Dada were bitter political enemies, but I don't think he would kill Dada. He's not that sort of man. I'd trust him with my life."

"Don't say that," she said.

"Why?" I asked.

"Do you really know him? My father doesn't trust anyone, and I think I've taken my cue from him. He says that being a policeman all his life taught him that anyone is capable of doing anything."

That was not how I saw things but I didn't say this to Nicole.

I looked over to the Hope River and imagined what it would have looked like in my greatgrandfather's time. The aqueduct that carried water down to August Town would have been working, the waterwheel that had been destroyed in the fire would have been turned lazily by the water that now led into the reservoir. I told Nicole how it had been, how the river's only freedom now was where it seeped underground through the cracks in the mortar as it pushed against the wall of the aqueduct until it emerged in Legba's Claim. There among the thorns and thicket, it deposited its rich loam, nourishing whatever had seed or the urge to grow.

"You know," she said, "you've never told me how you ended up living in Jamaica with your father instead of with your mother in Miami."

"I don't like talking about it," I said.

"C'mon, Jason, you need to talk about it, especially now. Especially here."

She stood up and turned her back to me and leaned against my chest. She was wearing the perfume I'd given her for her birthday, Opium. I nibbled the hairs on her nape, the soft curls behind her ear, and held her around her waist.

"From what my mother told me, when he announced that he was going to marry Emma, she had a nervous breakdown. Later, he used that against her in court. He told the court that he could provide a more stable environment for the child, and they went along with him. That's how crooked the courts are in this country. Justice depends on who you know."

"Are you sure that's true?"

I undid the top button of her dress and slid my hand inside. Her bra felt warm against my palm. I reached for the clip.

She took my hand away from her bra, and bent over to fold up the chair. The cotton dress was crumpled around her buttocks. Nicole had the kind of buttocks that dance hall DJ's are forever rhyming about. Round and ample without the slightest trace of excess fat, they reminded me one of Basil's earliest works that I'd seen at the National Gallery in Kingston.

Fighting through the traffic, I'd gotten there ten minutes before closing time. The guards were just then slowly closing the windows and doors, but I had to finish my report for art class. I set out to convince a guard to let me in just to see that one piece. I must have looked harmless enough so he let me inside for a few minutes. At the furthest end of the gallery, I saw the sculpture, "Eve". It was a mahogany figure, about seven feet tall, with large breasts, full thighs, and the sort of buttocks that boys in boarding schools dream about.

Workers were busy cleaning the floors and dusting the sculptures. One of them, a small man, only about five foot, reached up as he was cleaning the sculpture and fondled its buttocks. "Sweet, sweet," he said. Talk about art for the masses.

Nicole leaned the chair against the railing and looked down at the river that spread like a dark fan across the mouth of the bay.

"Is that why you don't want to come back here?" she asked.

"We've had this discussion before," I said.

"I saw you this afternoon and I've just been listening to you. You know every stone, every rock, every tree."

She noticed I was looking down the front of her dress and

she turned away and smiled. She buttoned up her dress, concealing the tan line around her bra that went from mocha to toffee brown.

"I'm being serious, Jason," she said.

"And so am I."

"Not about that. At least, not now."

"So I have a chance," I said.

"Maybe," she said, teasing me. "If you behave yourself." Although we'd been together for almost a year, Nicole always wanted to be seduced before we made love. While it was at times tiring, the chase always made an elegant dance.

"Spark's honour," I said.

From the back of the house, the scent of gardenias seeped into the dark throats of orchids as they spread their lavender petals across their baskets suspended from the trunks of Australian pines.

"You know you belong here, don't you? Miami is no place for you."

"I met you there, didn't I, so it can't be all that bad."

"It's not right for you."

"It's not right for you either, but what are we going to do? That's where I live, that's where I work."

"You could leave that job. You could work somewhere else. We could live here?"

"And do what? Telemarketing is the only work I really know how to do."

"Don't sell yourself so cheaply, Jason. You're a lot stronger than you give yourself credit. There are lots of things I know that you can do if you put your mind to it."

"Such as?"

"Your drawing."

"Second rate stuff."

"Says who?"

"All the people who really know about art."

"Yes, but do they really care about you? With your education and your intelligence, you could work anywhere."

"How do you know that?"

"I saw how you handled your mother's funeral arrangements. Sure, Trevor helped you, but you did a lot of that alone. But you have to stop punishing yourself over her death, there was nothing more you could have done about it."

I didn't want to talk about this any more. We'd been having such discussions ever since I confessed to her what I did for a living. I had to. Nicole worked as the branch manager for Nations Mortgage, a major firm with its headquarters in Orlando, and she was determined to break through the glass ceiling. The president, William Foster, proclaimed his liberal leanings and said he was willing to promote her as far as she wanted to go. Nicole wanted to go far.

When I'd first met her she was walking around the Warner Pavilion of Mt. Sinai Hospital. Her father was being treated for lung cancer and I'd seen her pacing the halls, usually before I slipped in to see my mother. Sometimes she walked right past my door and I became aware of the particular sounds her shoes made against the matting.

"You walk like a duck," I said and it caught her off-guard.

"I beg your pardon," she said, turning on her middle-class Jamaican accent that should have frozen any further advances from forward men.

"I said you walk like a duck."

She burst out laughing. "You know you're the only man, with the exception of my father, who's told me that."

"He must love you a lot," I said, getting really forward. "Hi, my name is Jason Stewart."

From then on, I used to tease her and call her the duck lady. We'd meet downstairs for a snack and walk out to the bay in between our parents' chemotherapy sessions. Nicole went with me to see my mother in her last days. But I never went with her to see her father. At least, not until he was fully recovered and back on his feet.

When it came time to bury my mother, Nicole helped me to put together the money for the funeral and I confessed at this point that I was a telemarketer. At first, she was upset because I had deceived her. I'd told her the usual lie about retail marketing. On the day of my mother's funeral, we made up, but she still didn't like what I was doing.

"Even if we came back here to live what would you do? How could I support you?"

"I don't need you to support me, Jason. I can take care of myself."

I turned away from her and faced the gully. Kingston flickered through the pine needles, a quilt of light and darkness.

"And you can't go on with the lies," she said, and ran her hand along the railing. Her fingers were long and fine, the nails painted a deep burgundy colour.

"What lies?" I said.

"The lies, Jason. The phone scams everyday. You can't lie everyday and not have it affect your life."

"What are you talking about?"

"I talked with Trevor," she said. "He told me."

"He's not in jail?"

"He's not in jail? What are you talking about, Jason?"

"Nothing."

I held my head down, then tried to follow with my eyes a footpath that led through Legba's Claim, through the swamp and behind Wareika to Rockfort.

"Come on, tell me," she said.

"Trevor could be in jail," I said. "He hit a cop."

"So you didn't think to tell me before?"

"No, it's not that simple. I'm involved."

Nicole bit her lips until they turned white. She buttoned up her dress all the way, turned her back to me and gazed down at the back yard, the copse, then and the hills. I'd never seen her so angry in my life.

"I can't believe it," she said. "You were involved?"

"Not really," I said. I had wanted to wait to break the news to her as gently as possible, but now it was all going out of control.

"How could you do this to me, Jason? How could you get

involved in something like that? Do you know what my father would do if he found out – and he will – that you were involved in something like this?"

"I was going to tell you," I said.

An egret tucked its legs under its body and climbed lazily out of the swamp. Its wings seemed luminous in the darkness.

"When? When were you going to tell me? I can't believe you got yourself into something like this. What's even worse, I can't believe you'd leave your friend, who's seen you through your mom's funeral and everything, like that."

"I just needed time to think this through," I said defensively.

"This isn't thinking, Jason. This is doing or not doing. You left your friend when he needed you. Would you do the same to me, Jason? Suppose I told you I was pregnant, what would you do?"

"Are you?"

"That's not the point! I want to know if I found myself in situation that I didn't know what to do, would you run away like you did with Trevor?"

"I'd never leave you like that!"

"How do I know that? What's wrong with you? This is not the Jason that I came down from Miami with!"

"Well, if you didn't come down to Jamaica with me, you might as well leave," I said, then realized how stupid I was. But there was no turning back.

"Maybe you're right," she said. "Maybe you're right. I think you'd better leave my room."

"I think I will," I said. "I think I will."

CHAPTER FIVE

"David Carmichael... He's your man," blared the graffiti along Hope Road. The boulevard was blockaded with overturned trucks, torched cars and barbed wire. We had to walk through the back of Standpipe to get to JC. Tony and I stood in the middle of the burned-out tract between the college and Standpipe, and gazed at broken shanties and gutted tenements.

I had awakened that Saturday morning to hear Chris telling me that Nicole had already left for the airport with Cedrick. I knew she was angry, but angry enough to leave? My first reaction was to drop everything and chase after her, but I decided that if she was so upset, I'd better give her some time to cool off before I saw her again. It would give me enough time to come up with a new story. I was good at such things, making up good stories to match a bad situation and make everything seem all right.

But I suppose I wasn't that surprised that she'd left. People were always leaving me to take care of their own lives. All I ever wanted was to live like everyone around me. In Miami I saw people leading happy everyday lives. I saw them on the highway talking on their cell phones, going to the beach, to work, to Bayside. I saw them in the malls holding hands with their loved ones, their children, and I thought: Why can't I be one of these lucky people? What's stopping me from parading around with a smile on my face?

Nicole was right. The job was eating away at my insides. I hated the daily manipulation of people for money. But what else could I do? I lived in a country where my worth was calculated by the size of my credit card debt. Would she really stay with me if I didn't have a job or money?

But for now I had to postpone these questions. Chris had to take care of a broken water main at the hotel and had already left, so Tony and I had to borrow Emma's Land Rover. Trini dropped us off at the border and told us he'd pick us up in two hours because Emma wanted to go to Sabina Park for the start of the test match.

Emma and Dada went to every match at Sabina. Emma loved cricket. I used to play the game, but never liked it. I usually felt out of it, stuck on the boundary with red ants crawling over my white gear. It seemed to go on for days. For me, it was a game of personal ambition masquerading as a team sport. There were no sacrifices, as in baseball or soccer, where you put your body or your batting average on the line for the team. In cricket you guarded your wicket like an animal guarding its territory and you had to stay inside your crease. And you never, never, never used anything else but your bat to defend your wicket. To do otherwise violated the rules and spirit of the game. We Jamaicans had a passion for cricket, with all its rules and order, when order and predictability were the things this country sorely lacked. It was another contradiction in a country filled with contradictions.

Tony and I walked past the rows of barbed wire and barricades and headed into Standpipe. Normally our journey would have been impossible, but Chris, after negotiating with Carmichael, had gotten us clearance. Chris had told Carmichael that I wanted to retrieve Dada's plaque before I left, and played on the whole idea of tradition and Old Boy loyalty. I called Doc and told him I'd meet him at twelve in Scotland Hall, and he said he would be waiting for me in the biology lab.

Chris had convinced Carmichael that I would be safe because no one knew who I was. I was a returning visitor, neither JLP nor PNP, and I told them in advance what I would be wearing: sneakers, blue jeans, and a Dolphins T-shirt. All I needed was a camera to complete the impression that I was an American tourist. Tony, though, was wearing a Fila sweat suit; I didn't know how he could stand it in this heat.

A man was waiting for us at the furthest end of a field covered with broken glass, rusty cans, and spent shells. Shaka Zulu, as he called himself, one of Carmichael's generals, was built like a linebacker with enormous arms and thighs that bulged with muscles. He was dressed in full army fatigues, and was pointing a sawn-off shotgun at me.

The only time this had happened to me before was when I went with Dada to return some speakers to the party headquarters in Kingston. A young man had sneaked up on us as we were unloading the speakers from the trunk. Dada had his revolver in the trunk and could have shot the young man dead. No questions asked. Instead, he handed me the speaker and said to the young man, "You better know what you going do with a gun before you point it at someone," and turned his back.

The young man was rattled. He didn't know what to do. He ran off and we continued unloading the speakers.

"Weren't you scared?" I had asked.

"Always stand firm," Dada said. "Never let them see that you're scared or you may end up doing something you don't want to do. Then both of you could end up dead," and he closed the trunk of his car.

"You is the boy?" Shaka asked.

Tony stepped in front of me, squared his shoulders, and held a steady gaze at the man.

"Yes, Carmichael clear we. Him say we must ask for Shaka if we have any problems."

Shaka stepped back, "I man know you! What you doing here?"

"Don't make that worry you," said Tony. "Me passing through. We will meet you back here in two hour as we say on the phone."

"I man haffi check with the boss before you go any further. We never know it was going involve you," said Shaka.

"You going bother Carmichael for something as small as this? I man did think is you control? If Carmichael don't shit, you cyaan eat?"

"Watch you mouth, boy. You know is me control now. Is only respect. Nuff respect."

He lowered the gun, then waved his hand in the air, and two men with rifles, who were also in army fatigues and dark glasses, climbed down from a tamarind tree. One of the men, holding a transistor radio against his ear, was eagerly awaiting the start of the test match. Shaka signalled to a boy in a floral shirt and khaki pants with holes in the bottom who was playing bulldozer with a set of discarded dentures. The boy, small and thin, his legs covered with scabs, continued playing for a moment, then picked up some torn strips of red cloth and ran towards us. Behind him, an ackee tree in full bloom released its toxins into the air.

"Yes, Shaka, you want me?"

Shaka rapped the boy on the forehead with the handle of the shotgun, and the boy fell to the ground. The boy held his head and wriggled in the dirt. A spurt of blood from his nostrils stained his shirt. Shaka waited until the boy stopped crying, then crouched beside him. He held the boy's hand.

"Selly, when I give the signal, everybody must come, same time. No waiting business, no play business. You drop whatever you doing and come. Now, search them."

The boy, still whimpering, ran his hand along my waist, chest, back and around my ankles. The blood trickled over his trembling lips that were wet from his tears. He nodded to Shaka and searched Tony. He found a twenty-two calibre around Tony's ankles and ran over to Shaka with the gun.

Shaka had already lifted his gun to his waist and brushed the boy to the side. The men with the rifles aimed at us. I raised my hands over my head while Tony remained calm.

"What this? Is murder you come to murder somebody?"

asked Shaka. A bead of sweat ran down the front of his sunglasses

"Man, you know that is only a pea-shooter. It cyaan hurt a soul," said Tony.

"You did really think you could come in here with that?"

"I carry it in case something should happen."

"Nothing going happen while you is here. I feel to turn you back pan you Labourite raas and send you back where you come from."

"If you do that," said Tony, "then you going have to tell Carmichael why."

Pulling the boy to his side, Shaka searched for the bruise on his forehead, then kissed him where he had bruised him.

"You see what I mean, son. You did think that him never have no gun, but see, you see. If we don't corporate, we would dead. Him could have killed me, and you wouldn't have no father. What you would do after that?"

"I understand, Shaka," said the boy. "I won't do it again."

"That good," said Shaka. "Now you have something for me?"

Selly ran over to the spot where he had fallen and picked up the strips of cloth. He handed the strips to Tony, then stood behind Shaka.

"Tie them around you arm, and make sure you don't lose them. Is your only protection while you is here. We will meet back here in one hour. If you don't come back, then you on you own. And if we haffi come get you, is a different story. You got that?"

"We got it," said Tony.

The two men with the rifles approached and led us through the outskirts of the town. Broken glass crackled under our soles. The sun had peeled the paint off the sides of the tenements and exposed the raw nakedness of the wood. My eyes were drawn to a large concrete house, a monstrosity of a rectangular box with a satellite dish on the roof, shaded but not disguised by the leaves of a breadfruit tree.

"Who lives here?" I asked.

"Shaka," said Tony.

"Where did he get the money to build a house like this in Standpipe?"

"This is all cocaine money, but he can't live nowhere else. Outside of Standpipe him cyaan live in peace. Him would have the house, but him would always have to be on guard. Here in Standpipe him can leave him front door open."

The men left us on a washout overlooking Standpipe. The thatched huts and tin shanties wrapped themselves around the hillside, circles and circles of mud, plywood and zinc that exposed the limestone underbelly yellowed by the sun.

"Did you know that guy back there? He sounded as if he didn't like you."

"You right him don't like me. Him think me is a traitor."

"A traitor? Why?"

"Five year ago Shaka burn down a whole part of August Town that did vote against Carmichael after them cut into Standpipe. When me mother find out that we under PNP rule, we move full full into August Town. You father get her a house in a housing scheme down there. You remember my mother?"

"Yes, what happened to her?"

"She wanted to go to the States to work, so you father set her up in New York. She working as a maid for some rich white people. She say she might write a book."

"A book about what?"

"The slackness of white people." He chuckled to himself as we descended through a washout strewn with plastic bags. A flock of John Crows, mobile black dots, hovered over the carcasses of dead dogs while others swooped down, then climbed into the upper blue, gliding on the air currents that lifted them higher and higher into the sky.

Standpipe was a gangrenous artery of Kingston. Lives oozed in and out, clogged between the splintering light that fell through the tamarind trees to the rubbish-strewn ground and the aerial spiral of the John Crows who, like gregarious mutes, remained detached from the heat.

Thank God Nicole had left. I'd put this side of the island out of my mind, and if she'd been here she would have wanted to come no matter how dangerous the trip sounded.

I was still angry with her though. *I don't need you to support me, Jason. I can take care of myself.* I know that. I've always known that. All of the women that I've known from my mother to Emma knew how to take care of themselves. What I meant was, where did I fit in her life? But it didn't come out that way. She hadn't given me a chance to explain my side of the story. That it was Trevor, after he had knocked out the cop, who had told me to run.

At least, that was what I was going to tell her. About our reason for being there, I'd remain silent. I was going to tell her that the cop was going to shoot us, and we acted only in self-defence. And if anyone took the time to listen to us, they'd see our side of the story. After all, we were in Miami.

"I heard Emma and Chris arguing again this morning. What was it about this time?"

"The usual," said Tony, "but you will find out soon enough. Your father leave all him money to Miss Emma. Him did afraid you brother would throw her out in the streets, so after she dead you two can share everything between you."

"Who says I want any of my father's money?"

I was lying, but he didn't deserve to be told the truth. But wasn't this just another excuse?

"You brother wants his share and him say him going fight it in the court," said Tony.

"And he'll win. Poor Emma."

Between the hunched shoulders of the hills what was left of Hope River trickled through the shanties. Across from the wooden walkways, a boulevard separating the residential and the commercial area ran straight into New Kingston. Jitneys, overflowing with passengers hanging from the sides and the tops, sped past the bus stops.

"Hey, red man! Want a piece of this. Twenty American dollars for a taste."

Approaching us was a woman with a red-haired wig and red sequined dress, waving to me. Emaciated and worn, her skin had the colour of the pavement. She sashayed up the boulevard in her black stilettos, and when she snapped her fingers, her bangles clanged against each other.

"Wasn't that the woman they arrested at the funeral yesterday?"

"Yeah, that's the one and only Pearl Harbor. She drunk already."

"Pearl Harbor? Why do they call her that?"

"Your father give her the name. Him said she used to work the docks and she drown a whole heap of sea men."

That sounded like Dada. He and Doc were famed for their bad puns.

"How come she's out of jail already?"

"They have more to worry about than to put a old whore in a lock up. Why waste jail space and food on her."

Pearl Harbor lifted her skirt above her waist and skipped over a row of periwinkles that grew in cracks in the pavement. She was carrying a plastic bag with her clothes from the day before that she held carefully, so when she swung it from side to side she wouldn't break her pink neon fingernails. Then she stood her ground defiantly, arms akimbo, and started to grind her hips.

"For you red man, ten American dollars, ten."

I couldn't resist. I had to ask Tony. "Dada ever sleep with her?"

"No," said Tony and shook his head. He seemed surprised that I'd ask such a question. "Him had more sense than that. Him feel sorry for her more than anything else. She come from a good family and one time she did own her own house and land, but rum take away everything. So you father used to help her out every Christmas at the family planning clinic to get herself tested every now and then." He stooped and picked up a handful of stones. "We don't want what you have," shouted Tony. "You too old, with your shrivel up pum-pum."

"Oh, is you," screamed Pearl Harbor. "I not talking to you, you little blood claat. I talking to him, the red man."

"Have some respect leggo beast. This is not no tourist. This is Mr. Lumley son who come from Miami for the funeral."

"Kiss me raas. You is Jason! You is the one from Miami him always talking about? Then, boy, you can get it for five dollars. Cheap, cheap. What you say to that? Don't fraid, pum-pum won't bite. I promise you. It sweet like sugar. Sweet, sweet. Sweet like molasses."

"No, thanks," I shouted.

She rocked her waist from side to side. "Cheap, cheap and nothing sweeter than this. If you father was alive, him would tell you the same."

So this was what my father, a symbol of our island's history, had come to: consorting with women who sold their bodies for American dollars. So much for our illustrious past. We'd forgotten, despite the horror and the beauty, all this was ours. Without that everything else became meaningless, reduced to the lowest common denominator – pum-pum for sale – everyone could agree on that.

Tony grabbed me by the arm and led me down a street by the corner of a grocery store where a group of men passed their days racking up scores of victories in domino games and an equally impressive amount of baby mothers. The store was barricaded and the windows grilled with wrought iron bars.

I recognized the store. Larry, Damien and I used to sneak away from JC by crawling down the old aqueduct behind Hardy House and come here to buy patties, plantain tarts, and cigarettes. When we were older, we bought beer, wine and rum. The owner, Chung-Fah, was a swarthy, overweight Chinese man who, Damien said, seduced schoolgirls by giving them icy mints. In those days, this part of Standpipe was neutral territory. Chung-Fah had been JLP. I guessed he must have made his accommodation.

The domino players sat on wooden crates outside the store, while an old man, fiddling with the dial of a transistor radio, slouched by the door. He was alternately tracing along his bare gums with his fingers and scratching his neck. A neon sign over his head blinked, "Coke Adds to Life!"

The doors of the grocery store swung open and bumped the old man. He fell and rolled into the gutter. Chung-Fah chupsed while the old man tried to regain his spot.

"Egbert, you wretch you. Every morning is the same thing, eh. Why you don't find somewhere else to kotch a morning time so me no haffi bounce you outta de way."

Egbert didn't complain. This was how each day found him, a daily bounce to remind Chung-Fah that he was still around. At first Chung-Fah didn't recognize me because the last time he saw me, I'd had a full beard and moustache in sixth form. He held out his hand.

"Jason, boy, good to see you."

I shook his hand. He had refused my hand thirteen years ago after I had broken completely with my father and told him he was supporting the wrong people. I told him that the JLP was only supporting the wealthy people in Jamaica and I wouldn't be a part of it. Carmichael, I asserted, with his own poultry business, would never want to take over small private businesses to be run by the state, but everyone knew he admired the reforms in education and medicine that Fidel had brought about in Cuba. If your baby has whooping cough, you don't care what kind of doctor will treat the child, Cuban or otherwise. You just want a doctor. Or the devil himself.

Then to further anger both him and my father, I attended a political rally in the PNP heart of Standpipe where Fidel Castro planted a mango tree. The JBC covered the event and my father was deeply embarrassed to see me on the platform with Basil Cunningham. The mango tree died a few years later.

"I sorry to hear about you father. I really sorry about that. I did want to go, but Verna, because she used to work for your old man, was the only one them let pass through yesterday."

"I know, I saw her," I said. "I waved to her, but she didn't see me."

"Couldn't see you," he said. "She sick, sick bad. Rum eat out the whole of her belly. They say she soon dead, so I guess that's why them let her out to your father funeral. But is a good thing I see you today. Come inside and talk with me. I have something to tell you."

I was about to go inside when Tony said, "We don have the time. We cyaan stay."

Chung-Fah kissed his teeth. "One minute," he said. He guided me inside the store and closed the door. If Tony didn't like Chung-Fah, that was reason enough for me to go with him. Chung-Fah had simple passions and maybe he could help me to understand the swirl of events happening around me. Maybe I could get some information out of him without revealing anything about myself. It was the safest way for now.

The smell of cod, red herring, and salt pork mingled with the rank stench of raw sewage that penetrated everywhere.

"Watch you back with that boy," said Chung-Fah, "him dangerous."

"My brother sent him with me as protection."

"Better you carry a snake in your bosom." So far, I was right about one thing. But Tony hadn't liked me then and he didn't like me now. So that was no big deal.

Chung-Fah took me into the back of the store, past the shelves filled with rows and rows of Kellogg's, Quaker Oats, bottles of Horlicks, and tins of Milo and Ovaltine, cans of all shapes and sizes, green, brown, and dark coloured bottles with thick syrupy liquids and clear round bottles with honey and jams. During the elections that drove Carmichael from office, all of these had been scarce goods, yet every Friday evening we had all the groceries we wanted delivered to the back door of our house. Emma would pay cash.

"So how you mother? She come down for the funeral too?"

"She died a year ago."

"I sorry to hear that, but since the war it hard to get news any more. But make we get down to business. I have something to tell you, but not here."

The walls inside the office were covered with posters of nude Chinese women, and in the corner, beside a single bed, was a television set and a VCR with stacks of X-rated videos. This was the first time I'd been in the old sybarite's den.

"I fix up this place back here. The wife in Miami, so it get a lonely, you know what I mean," he said apologetically. "I've been waiting for you to come. Your friend says to tell you that plans changed. Him say to meet him at the tuck shop at JC."

"You know Adrian?"

"Yes. Make we just say that him used to do me some favours. Is the least I can do for him before I leave the island."

"You're leaving?" I couldn't believe this. Chung-Fah had been in Standpipe before it had a name. Standpipe grew up around his grocery store. If his business failed, the people who lived from day to day, from week to week, particularly those who lagged behind the week's wages, would be dealt another blow. His store had kept the place alive, and he extended credit to those he thought would repay him. The supermarkets never offered credit.

"I stay too long already," he said. "I should have left after I had to close down the patty shop. Everything changing. Burger King, McDonald's, Kentucky Fried Chicken, American fast food putting me out of business. The best place, my son tells me, to sell Jamaican food is in Miami."

"But what will happen to Standpipe? The people who depend on you?"

"These young boys who they deporting back from the States where they learn the real Mafia business, killing us with extortion and kidnapping. They have nobody here, so they just kill and murder without thinking. In the old days, the politicians use to be able to control people like that, but not anymore. Not even Carmichael can control his people anymore. They say him soft and can't chuck badness like him used to. And now that him kill your father..."

"You think Carmichael killed Dada?"

He pulled me over to his bed, put a tape in the VCR and turned up the volume on the television. A dark-haired, muscular man dressed up as a woman was applying for a job as a female wrestler. The promoter, a blond woman in a one-piece bathing suit with the Stars and Stripes emblazoned over the front, was looking over the new prospect. It was typical American porn. Like the descent of grace on the unworthy, or the unwatchful sinner being caught up in the rapture, sex could happen any time, anywhere.

"Everybody know that. Who else could do that and don't dead by now. One man and only one man could do it, and that man is David Carmichael. Your father collar him and him couldn't get away. Your father finally have him where only death could save him. That's why you father dead. I hope your brother win. I hope him win the election and cut we back into August Town."

The wrestler was demonstrating a hold on the promoter. He pinned her to the carpet, exposing her breasts, but she shook her head. He was obviously an amateur.

I knew Chung-Fah had his own motives for saying Carmichael was the killer. He had been in league with all the other merchants who had driven Carmichael from power. But what if he was telling the truth?

"So you think my brother will win?"

"Who better to take over from your father?"

I shifted my eyes back to the television. The promoter showed the man a move of her own. The man was impressed. The promoter took the man upstairs to show him some more moves.

"With your father gone, Carmichael will rule. If that happen again, I gone."

"But what are you going to do in Miami?"

"My son say we can open a store and sell the same thing

as I doing here. I will miss this place, but I have to think about me life. They say Miami is like Jamaica. Is true?"

"Almost," I said. "Almost."

He turned off the television and the VCR and waddled back to the front door. He opened the door. The crowd had grown larger.

"I don't know why the whole of you standing up out here in the hot sun," he said. "Everything short. Flour short, rice short..."

"Pum-pum short?" shouted a man at the back.

"That never short in Jamaica," said Chung-Fah and he picked up his broom. "Jason," he said, "you should really go look for Verna before you leave. She will be really glad to see anybody from your family. The whole of her belly rotten out. She never forgive Emma when she turned her out the house for stealing your father rum. When she couldn't afford regular liquor, she drink bay rum. And now see what happen. She going dead from all them years of rum drinking and hard life. And she was so pretty. You must go look for her."

"I must see her then," I said. "I'll see you."

"Soon, boy," he said, tucking his shirt in his pants and tightening his belt over his sagging belly.

Whackata, whackata, whackata. A domino game was ending and tiles were flying everywhere.

One of the players had risen to his feet and was taunting the player sitting across the table, "Me a de gorgon you hear me. Me a de gorgon. Cho, man, play your card! Chisel, play your card. Just come in like me and my girl, Susan. Every time we make love, me go in like a boss, for she is a mule. Hood the boy like him is a virgin child!"

The player was showing the three things you needed to play dominos in Jamaica: luck, skill, and a big man swagger to go with these qualities. You needed luck to draw the right tiles and skill to turn the game around even if you didn't draw a good hand. By playing your tiles in the right sequence, your partner could read or figure out the cards in your hand and play the right cards so you could get rid of all your cards and vice versa. A good domino player was part mathematical genius and part obeah man. And a strong arm, so that when you bowed your hand, slapping the cards on the table to sound like thunder, like the old ballers used to do, "Heineken, Heineken, Heineken, Heineken," it didn't hurt.

Chisel, who must have got his name from the shape of his forehead, picked up and rearranged the dominoes in his hand. He squeezed the tip of the cap he was wearing, shifted on the crate, and then played a domino he had been keeping under his leg.

"Duffus, me pardy, don't know about you and your girl friend, but I going harden this boy heart till him get a heart attack."

Chisel played an ace blank. Duffus, a barrel-chested man picked up the domino off the table. Blank deuce faced Duffus.

"This is the raas claat card I been waiting for, you old miser," he said lifting his leg as he farted.

Duffus showed the card to everyone and then held three dominoes in this hand. He pounded the domino on the table and Chisel smiled.

"Now this boy, him pass like raas, and when," he said to the man on his right, "when I play this card, you, Mr. Snapper, haffi play deuce four up at that end, for this blank harder than my hood. That was the card I was waiting for. You holding it like it was some virgin that don't want to have its cherry busted. But bring it here, bring it right here, for the cherry busters are here. Right here! Whoop, whoop, whoop!"

Snapper put his dominos on the table, got up and kicked away the crate he was sitting on. His partner got up with him and disappeared into the crowd.

"Where de raas you doing?" Duffus grabbed Snapper before he could leave. "What de raas you doing?"

"The game over," said Snapper and pushed Duffus away from him.

"All right then," said Duffus. "If the game over, then pay up. You owe me ten dollars, pay up."

"I not paying you nothing," said Snapper, and he pursed his lips. "You and your partner is a set of thief. I work too hard for my money, and you never work a day in your life. All you do is live with them thiefing politician. But I not going let you thief my money."

"You hear that," said Chisel, "him call you a thief."

"Pay up, pay up," said Duffus. "You owe us ten dollars. You lose the game."

"I not paying you a fucking farthing. You and your partner been robbing me all morning. Oonu is thief!"

The crowd, sensing danger, parted in front of Snapper. Duffus drew his ratchet and charged. He held Snapper against the wall, and the crowd surged back to see what would happen next. Tony and I were trapped in the middle, unable to move.

"Who the bumbo claat you calling a thief?" Duffus held the knife to Snapper's throat.

"I finally figure it out," Snapper said. "It did take me time, but I figure it out."

"Figure out what?" Duffus loosened his grip around Snapper's throat.

"I figure it out," said Snapper. "When ever you talk about your virgin girl, it mean your partner must play blanks. I figure it out. You think I don't hear code when I hear one."

"Which code?"

This was serious. It was the ultimate insult.

"Chisel was going play deuce ace. But when you say draw ducks with your girl friend, him play blanks. You think me is a fool. Ducks mean blanks. I been playing dominos too long for someone like you to thief me."

Duffus grinned. "You don't prove nothing. That don't prove a thing. Pay me my money"

"I not paying you a fucking farthing. I don't play with thief."

"Him call you a thief again, Duffus," said Chisel.

"You right," he said, "you right. Him disrespect my name and him going to have to pay the price for that."

As Snapper turned to appeal to the crowd, Duffus drew his ratchet and stabbed him in the back. By the time Snapper was facing Duffus he had drawn his own knife and he cut Duffus across the chest. As if shocked at what he had done, Snapper dropped his knife and reached out his hand to Duffus' chest as if to staunch the wound.

"No, don't wipe it away. Make it stay right there. You say me is a thief, so make we see if I can thief it off your face before it dry."

Duffus threw his ratchet to Chisel and picked up Snapper's knife. He raised it to his mouth and licked the blood off it.

"This is my blood. My blood! When my mother piss me into this world, she never send me to get cut by a shit like you. And she never send me for you to call me a thief either. Look around you, you see all the money you have. I don't want it. You insult me."

Duffus braced Snapper against the wall again and popped the buttons off his shirt with the knife. He turned to crowd, "Ladies and gentle man of the jury. You see how this boy disrespect my name. How you find him, guilty?"

The crowd murmured a tentative assent, anxious to see what would happen next.

"All right, Duffus," said Snapper, "I call you a thief and I sorry. If that is what you want me to say, I say it. But if is beg you want me to beg for me life, me not going do it."

"Now you calling me a murderer. Boy, when you going stop disrespect me!"

Duffus turned to the crowd and made circular motions with his hands. He creased his pants, straightened his collar and held Snapper's face to the crowd.

"You have heard the accused call me a thief and now he has called me a murderer. You all know I am a innocent man who wouldn't hurt a gingy fly. To prove my case I will call on Mr. Chisel."

Chisel brought one of the crates they had been sitting on and took a race form from his back pocket and gave it to Duffus. Chisel stood on the crate, raised his right arm and placed his left hand on the top of the race form that Duffus now held.

"Do you swear to tell the truth, the whole truth, and nothing but the truth, Mr. Devine?"

"I, Chisel Devine, do solemnly swear to tell the truth, the whole truth and nothing but the truth, so help me My Girl in the trifecta this evening."

"Mr. Chisel, you have been sworn in. I only have one question. You ever see me kill anybody without just cause?"

"No, Mr. Duffus."

"That is all. Thank you, Mr. Chisel."

Chisel stepped off the crate and winked at Snapper. The sun was directly in Snapper's eyes, but he didn't move his hands. He batted his eyelids, but the strain was too great, so he closed his eyes. Duffus grabbed him by the hair and slapped him on the side of the head.

"Don't fall asleep. You on trial!"

The crowd jeered as Snapper was forced to kneel at Duffus' feet. Duffus winked at Chisel as he rocked Snapper's head back and forth.

"Ladies and gentle man of the jury. You have heard the testimony of the accused. What say you?"

"Guilty," said Chisel.

"What is the punishment?" asked Duffus.

"Corner him little bumbo claat and thump him," screamed a voice from the crowd.

"I going do better than that," said Duffus. "A man name is the only thing in this world that him have, and is the only thing that left after him dead. A man haffi defend him name. Calling me a murderer!"

"I never call you a murderer!"

"Too late, too late. The court will hear no late submissions, no pleas for mercy. We have already come to a decision based on the testimony we have heard. It has been decided that since one Snapper Smith has defamed the character and integrity of the plaintiff, Duffus O' Riley, by assuming he could not draw ducks with a certain girl child, who shall remain nameless at this point, and did further conspire to defraud the plaintiff of ten dollars, the court has decided the following punishment."

Duffus lifted Snapper to his feet. He turned again to the crowd, closed the ratchet and in the split second that Snapper thought he could get away, Duffus opened the ratchet again and wheeled in like a dervish.

Sunlight bounced off the blade as he plunged the knife into Snapper's groin. Snapper fell against a fence. Duffus unzipped his pants and pissed on his face.

I couldn't stand by and watch him being humiliated.

"That's wrong!" I cried out and, without thinking, I rushed over to Snapper's side. Chisel tripped me and I fell beside Snapper. His body was convulsing and his pupils were constricted to pin points.

Duffus zipped up his pants and bent over my chest. He rested the ratchet on my nose. He noticed the cloth around my arm and said, "Who the fuck asked you?"

He picked me up and pinned me against the zinc fence, pushing the knife in my face. "You want me cut you like me cut him?"

Tony came over to my side. "Is a youth from Miami," he said. "Him soft. Him don't know the runnings."

Duffus closed the knife again. "Don't try to be a hero, boy. Mind your own fucking business, stay out of black people business." And he slapped my head to make his point.

He waved to Chisel and the two of them headed down the lane. Duffus' shirt was a bloody rag.

"You trying to dead?" Tony asked.

"I was trying to help."

"That's not how you help."

"But that man..." Snapper was writhing in the dust and grinding his teeth, "needs our help."

"You stay out of it," he said. "This is not August Town. You can get killed for trying to help. Keep out of their business."

"But he needs someone to help him."

"Look, you're an American tourist here. That makes you the biggest target. Trust me and do things my way so the two of we don't dead. I want to get out of this place alive. Leave him alone and come with me. Besides him deserve whatever him get, him own partner, that traitor, leave him like that. Him deserve to dead."

When he said that, I thought of Trevor. Had I deserted him to a similar fate? And Tony was right; I just didn't want to admit it. I had no business putting my nose where I didn't belong. But then I'd been accused of doing that all my life.

As we walked down the lane that led to Jamaica College a local sound system was warming up. The speakers crackled with roots reggae.

"Brothers and sisters, good day," said the DJ, "hope you feeling fine. Now here comes a pick of the past that I'm sure is gonna break your heart."

All I know, is I love you, sang Delroy Wilson, so confident about his love, *and if I live forever, I'll be loving you still.*

I was out of breath. We had been walking quickly and I held onto a fence post covered with posters announcing a dance with Stone Love at the controls. It would be a night of belly grinds with women in pum-pum shorts dubbing to the eternal strains of "Queen Majesty" while the smoke coiled around bodies slumped between a dozen eighteen inch speakers throbbing a bass line that would take away the pain.

"Slow down," I said. "I can't go any further. My heart is beating too fast."

"Is all the pork you been eating in America," said Tony. He was beginning to annoy me now. "But we can stop if you tired."

The sun hovered over the houses and dust hung in the air. Children scampered like rats through the holes in the fences, their screams bounced off the corrugated zinc.

"I hope you learn from what happen back there," he said.

"Okay," I said. "Next time..."

"We might not get a next time," he said curtly.

"Can we get off this," I said. "I want to visit Verna. I saw her yesterday. It will just be a quick stop."

"Over there," he said pointing to a guinep tree. "If we pass through the market, we can get to her house. But why you so anxious to see her?"

There was something about the way he said this that seemed to be more than a simple enquiry, though what he knew or what he was getting at I couldn't guess.

I had my reasons for wanting to see Verna, but Tony was the last person I would tell.

CHAPTER SIX

The market was jammed with higglers selling guavas, mangoes, naseberries, star apples and jackfruit. Sparks rustled under boiling pots and market women sat over wood fires breathing life into the embers. The noise from the market grew louder and higglers with baskets balanced on their heads came into the square. Buses belched black smoke into air already clouded with the smell of onion and garlic, fritters frying in coconut oil, the smell of thyme.

Cut off from the rest of the world, Standpipe was its own universe. Life continued no matter what was happening in the rest of the island.

Along the side of the road, women spread papayas on crocus bags, split, sliced and as inviting as their laughter, trying to outbid each other for a sale. Sharp whistles from the peanut vendor, an ugly man with a carbuncular nose, spiralled over the voices of the women. He chewed on a coconut shell that resembled a skull.

Mange-ridden dogs ran in and out of the stalls tumbling tables of yam, bananas and dasheen behind them. A higgler picked up an old shoe and hit one of the dogs in the side. The dog whimpered and ran through the legs of a girl who was arguing with a woman old enough to be her mother.

"I never tell you to stay away from him, eh? I never tell you?" said the older woman. She was dressed in a tattered blue frock, with orange rollers and a red Afro pik that resembled a rooster's comb stuck in her hair. She pulled at the girl's hair and the girl's blond wig came off in her hand. The girl, small and thin with fine East Indian features, tried to run, but the older woman caught her by the back of her blouse and clubbed her in the neck with her fist.

"Lawd, Miss Blossom, I never know this would happen. I never know!"

"Sssst. But I warn you. I warn you don't it. One used wig for sale!"

Miss Blossom stomped on the wig, grabbed the belt of the girl's skirt and tugged at the waist. The girl lurched forward and tried to protect her stomach with her hands.

"Lawd, Miss Blossom don't lick me in me belly. I pregnant."

"Pregnant? What pregnant have to do with anything? You think you is big woman? Big woman can take licks. My granny always say those who cyaan hear, must feel."

Miss Blossom tripped the girl and she fell to the ground. She ripped off the girl's blouse, then her brassiere. She tore at the girl's skirt and poked holes in the brassiere cups. The ugly man jumped to his feet and jabbed at the air, first an uppercut, then a left cross. He motioned to a higgler who was selling roasted yams and she nodded her head.

"Fight, fight and the winner gets me!" the ugly man shouted and beat his chest. The women ignored him.

"Pretty dress, pretty dress. Buying you pretty dress when me wearing this piece of cloth for ten years now. Pretty dress."

She slashed at the girl's stomach with her nails and didn't stop until she drew blood on her smooth skin. The girl tried to roll way, but Miss Blossom followed her and kicked the girl in the stomach. She kicked her. She kicked her again and again. I'd never seen women fight like that.

"Three month now and all him bringing home from work is change," said Miss Blossom. "The little that we have, him out spending it on you. I could understand rum, I could understand gambling. But this, this? Pretty dress?"

So that was it. Miss Blossom's man had a steady job and that was gold and the younger woman was about to get it all. Forget the niceties of no-fault divorce; it was red tooth and claw. As the old songs went, "only the fittest of the fittest will survive." Miss Blossom was a survivor.

The ugly man forgot his peanuts and passed a hundred dollars to the higgler who was selling roasted yams. The higgler smiled when she got the money.

Miss Blossom didn't stop until the girl had stopped moving, then tore what was left of the skirt off the girl's body. She shredded the skirt with her hands, and the seams she couldn't tear, she bit with her teeth. She trampled the wig one more time and walked away.

The girl lay motionless at the side of the road. The ugly man came over, took a look at her and shook his head, "You never put up a fight. You cost me a hundred dollars. Next time, fight the old *tegereg*! Don't be so *fenke fenke*. Put in two blows and keep your pride. If you lose, you still put up a good fight. You can't live in this island if you don't know how to chuck badness!" He scratched his head and walked away.

"And we walk by without doing anything?" I said.

"This is not our fight," Tony said.

"But don't you see, that's the whole problem?"

"You can't do nothing here unless you want to die for *these* people. Come with me if you want to live for another day. *This* not your fight."

"When will it be my fight?"

"It will never be here."

It was all so simple in his mind. Jamaica was divided into two sides and it would always be the same no matter what.

"But look, see," he said. "Verna house over there."

Verna's house stood in a lane surrounded by guinep trees. The house was fenced with barbed wire and impatiens grew around the posts. Some children were playing jump rope under an ackee tree.

"Room for rent, apply within. When I run out, you run in."

I walked up to the front of the house and knocked on the door while Tony waited under the ackee tree. The woman who was with Verna at the funeral met me at the door. She wore flowing white robes and a red tam. Her face was round and her eyes were deep set. The plainness of her dress against the ebony hue of her skin made her all the more beautiful – a true Rasta queen.

"Oh is you? What you want? Oonu cyaan make the woman dead in peace."

"Do I know you?"

"You is Albert Lumley son."

"Should I know you?"

"Know me? Why would you know me?" she said in a mocking tone.

A weak voice came out of the darkness. I peered over the woman's head, but I could only see the dim light of a kerosene lamp.

"Beryl, who that?"

"It's me, Verna," I said and I tried to enter the house. The woman barred the way. She put her hand on my chest and held on to the side of the door.

"What have I done to you? Why are you treating me like this?" I asked, taken aback by the force of her fury. I thought it was going to another of those brown/black animosities that I'd gone through all my life. Having to prove how black I was to my own people.

"Fuck you!"

The words exploded from her lips with a spray of saliva. I wiped the spit from my face.

"Beryl, make him come," pleaded Verna.

"But the doctor say no more excitement."

"Make him come," said Verna.

Beryl backed out of the doorway and I walked into the living room. I couldn't see too well because the windows had been covered with sheets.

"So you come to see the old girl," said Verna. "You can leave now, Beryl."

Beryl chupsed and left the room. I pulled up a chair beside Verna's bed. Over her head was a picture of Jesus of the Sacred Heart. The small night table on the other side of the bed was covered with *Watchtower* and *Awake* magazines. Under the kerosene lamp, the only light in the room, was a Gideon's Bible with a broken spine that was opened to Psalm Twenty-three.

Up close, she looked nothing like the Verna I'd remembered, who was the most beautiful woman I'd ever known. When she worked for us, I used to watch her leaning over the fence to pick mangoes or to talk with the other maids. She moved with an easy stride around the house like a panther on the prowl.

Verna held my hand and I moved closer. In the gloom I could barely see her face. A wiry clump of hair like a clump of Spanish needles seemed to pierce her scalp. Her skin was dry and ashen and covered with scaly shingles.

"How you doing, Verna?"

I couldn't bear looking at her. I could only hold her limp wrist in my hand.

"Not too bad, not too good," she said. "You have to forgive my youngest daughter, she trying her best to keep me alive."

"That's your daughter?"

That Verna could have a daughter my age would, at one time, have seemed impossible. Verna was Verna. She was mine.

"Yes," she said, then tried to raise her voice. "That's my RASTA daughter who won't go to church." She cut her eye at Beryl. "But you wouldn't know her. She was still child when you left."

"So why is she treating me like that?"

"She blame your family, especially Miss Emma, for me sickness, the drinking, the rum. But I try to tell her is me responsible. Me is a big woman. Me know what me was doing. Me can give it and me can take it, and me not too sick that me still can't give it."

91

A scent of urine and Bay rum escaped from under the sheets. I had to get up.

I released her hand and glanced around the room. A pale dull mirror that was losing its silvering was covered with Christmas cards that I'd sent her from Miami.

"You've kept all of them," I said.

"All," she said.

Under the mirror was a photo album. I opened the book. It was filled with photos and newspaper clippings that, though yellowed, were still preserved under plastic. Verna was always a pack rat.

In the middle of the book was a photo of my twelfth birthday. I had on a cowboy hat, and two toy guns hung down my sides. I looked as sullen as I did in all my other photos. In another photo, I was dressed as an Apache with war paint and tomahawk. Verna had a feather in her hair. I was still sullen.

Then I spotted the fake spider under a letter. She had kept that too. Verna was afraid of spiders and Chris had once hidden the spider under her soap dish.

Chris hated her because she had once spanked him, something that Dada had never done. Chris told Dada about it, and he said he would talk to Verna, but he never did anything. Chris didn't forget.

So one afternoon Chris came to me and said we should wait by the maid's quarters for a while. I asked him why and he said we'd soon see.

The next thing I knew Verna came screaming out of the shower wearing nothing but soapsuds. It was the first time I'd seen a naked woman. Chris was in stitches all afternoon, and though Dada punished him, he thought it was worth the punishment. Verna threatened to leave, but Dada pleaded with her to stay, and she agreed. Chris' allowance was suspended for three months and he was grounded for six.

The door squeezed open and Tony, covering his nose with his fingers, waved to me and said, "We have to go now," and went back into the living room.

I turned down the wick on the lamp and placed a fifty-dollar bill under the base. I left twenty dollars in my wallet.

"Take care of yourself," I said.

"Thank you my boy. Maybe it will help bury me."

"Don't talk like that."

"Is the truth. I soon gone."

"Well, if you need anything, anything at all, write to me in Miami," and I wrote: Jason Stewart, 1132 NW 32nd Avenue, Carol City, FL 33169 on the front of the *Watchtower* magazine. Verna looked at the name and shifted in the bed.

"So you still using the dead man name?"

"What?"

"The dead man, Neville Stewart, you still using him name? You still think that him is your real father?"

"I don't understand you."

"Look at the back of the album," she said.

I turned to the back of the album and found newspaper clippings about Dada and Carmichael: "Island-Wide Strikes. Lumley and Carmichael Call for Independence. Troops Called to End Riots. Governor-General Sets Date for First Election."

She had also collected stories from the gossip columns. I read for the first time the story about Dada's separation from my mother. The reporter from *The Star* took my mother's side. The story had pictures of Emma at New Year's parties, Christmas parties, each year with a different partner, her failed first marriage and a post election party with her hugging Carmichael.

And then I saw some papers that looked like a court transcript: "**** Lumley ***** blood test **** retain custody of the child, Jason Stewart. Lumley ***** child **** his. Myriam Lumley, former widow of ****** Neville Stewart, not to contest ******."

"I can't make this out," I said.

"Albert is your real father," she said. "When you mother left, she never want to take these papers, so I keep them."

I couldn't believe it. Had my mother been lying to me all

these years? It wasn't possible. Who was telling the truth? Everyone seemed to have their own version of my life that was totally at odds with what I knew about myself. My head was spinning.

"Can I keep this?" I asked her, and she said yes.

I peeled back the plastic and put the clipping inside my wallet. When I got back to Miami, I could photocopy and enlarge it to decipher the words. In the meantime, if anyone could help me sort through this, it would have to be Basil. He had dirt on everyone.

Tony slipped inside the room and tugged the back of my shirt. He held his fingers over his nose as he waited by the door.

"Verna, we have to go now," I said.

"I know. I happy for the short time you spend here. God bless you," she said.

As I turned to leave, she said, "Come over here, give me a kiss before you leave."

Tony left the room and went out into the yard. Verna drew back the sheets and the same rancid smell circled the room. Her lips were crusted with saliva.

"Jason, my sweet Jason," she said and she kissed me on the cheeks. "You must forgive you father for the sins that will send him to heaven."

The smell of the blankets rose up to my nostrils, and I felt as if I was choking. A foul smell curled out of the sheets and crept inside my shirt. I managed to kiss her on the forehead and patted her arm.

"My sweet, sweet boy," she said and squeezed my arm, like the first time we'd made love.

★★★

The summer after I passed my O Levels I was bored. Every Friday afternoon before Verna went home for the weekend, I'd wait by the curb for my friends from the block, Pat and David, to come up to my house and we'd cycle down to Mona Heights and play some three-a-side scrimmage soccer on the tennis courts. We'd known each other since we were children, but when we went to high school, we grew further and further apart. David went to Priory, where most of the diplomats' children went to school and after high school went to Sri Lanka to do research on his family history. Pat went to Campion, a Catholic high school, but later died in a car accident. We were a good team, and the other teams would wait for us to show up because we'd played so often together, we knew where to pass the ball without looking.

I had one eye on the road and one eye on the section of the maid's bathroom where the workmen had been adding a shower and new fixtures. I'd drilled a hole behind the cabinet while the workmen were on their lunch break and I was waiting for Verna to take a shower.

It was already four thirty when Pat and David rode up on their bicycles and I told them I'd meet them by the hockey field. David's girlfriend was on the hockey team, so I knew he wouldn't mind, and Pat loved to watch the girls in their mini skirts chase down the ball and sometimes get into scuffles.

Verna went inside the bathroom, and I told them I was going to get my bicycle. I ran around the back of the house where I normally parked my bicycle, then ran around the side to Verna's room.

She had already taken off her clothes when I got inside her room. I stood on the headboard, and watched her wash her hair, her neck, the soap foaming over her breasts, the dark aureoles. She rinsed the rag, washed her back and parting her legs, she washed her pubis, letting the water fall over her shoulders, buttocks and turned again to wash the soap off her stomach between her navel and pubic hair.

Then she started drying herself and threw her shirt over the hole. I didn't think she'd sensed my presence, so I continued looking through the hole, hoping she'd take down the shirt. Then I heard the door open behind me.

I jumped down off the headboard and tried to run through the side door, but she blocked me.

"Jason, if you did want to see me naked, why you never tell me?" The towel fell from around her breasts.

She climbed up on the bed and held me by the hand. I couldn't say anything. Verna put my hands on her breasts and then between her legs. She was still wet. Then, gently, she pulled down my shorts and jock strap and pulled me on top of her. Her belly was soft and warm and I was trembling all over.

I'd been watching her ever since Chris had played the trick on her. I watched her from my room, dressing and undressing, combing her hair, applying make-up and cleaning her face with Ponds. I'd wondered so many times what it would have felt like to be held in her arms, to caress her hair, and now I was inside her.

And it was over.

"Don't worry," she said. "Is your first time, nuh?"

"Yes," I said sheepishly

"Best is with me and not somebody else who going break your heart. If you want it to last though, you need to drink some rum. One sip, and it will make you last long. Bring some rum, as much as you can, next time."

From then on, every Friday, I stole a bottle of rum or any other liquor I could find in Dada's liquor cabinet behind the bar. We would drink whatever I could steal and that Dada wouldn't miss, then make love until about five thirty when she'd go home and I'd meet Pat and David and play the best soccer of my life.

***

I left the room and walked past Beryl sitting in the corner reading the Bible. Tony was standing out in the yard with his arms folded across his chest.

"Come on, Jason, give me a kiss. One kiss," he taunted. But this wasn't something new. He had always teased me when we were younger. "Where you mother, boy?" he would ask and then sing the lyrics to "Shame and Scandal", "Your daddy ain't your daddy, but your daddy don't know." I wanted to hit him, but I knew he was looking for an opportunity to pound me into the dirt. I left him alone.

"That's not funny, Tony. She's a sick, dying woman."

I tried to go through the gate, but he caught me by the elbow, and held my arm.

"Stop it," I said, tugging away from him. "I'm not feeling well."

"What wrong with you, boy?"

"I don't know," I said and pulled away from him.

"But you know enough to kiss old woman though," he said. "One kiss with tongue," he teased and puckered his lips.

"Get out of my way," I said. "The only thing I know now is that even you might be my brother," and pushed him out of my way.

A fist from my blind side knocked me to the ground. When I looked up Tony was glowering over me.

"Lawd man, look what *you* make me do!"

"What I made you do? What I made you do?"

Tony tried to help me to get up, but I wouldn't take his hand. I sat in the dust. I could taste the blood.

What had I been thinking, pushing him like that? It had been years since I'd been in a fistfight and he had been clawing his way through life from the time he was born. I had gotten slow.

"Let me help you up," he said.

"Get way from me!" I yelled.

"Don't tell me," he said sarcastically. "You going mad at me because of that bitch in there. Wha' make you think you special? You and your father was fucking her at the same time."

"What? How did you know that?"

"The hole you drilled over her bed. It work two ways, Jason," he said. He was always snooping around the house, in everyone's business. "I could see you, and especially your father, screwing all the maids. All you brown men are alike. Just like to fuck with black people pickney."

"Where do you get off calling me brown? We're all black! You never heard Peter Tosh sing, 'You're an African'."

"Song make for man to dance and rub girl to. Song don't make to live you life to! You is a idiot or something?"

I brushed the dust off my clothes and wiped my mouth with the cloth.

"How do I get to Jamaica College from here?"

"You can't go alone. Tie the cloth back around your arm."

I tied the cloth around my arm and said, "I don't want you near me."

"Don't make a woman come between us. I don't want to lose this job. Listen man, follow your father rule, the four Fs."

"The four Fs?"

"Yes," he said. "Find them, fool them, fuck them, and forget them. You can't make woman rule you!"

"That's where me, you, and my father part company. Bye, Tony."

"But," he said and tried to hold my arm again. I wriggled free of him.

"Don't worry about me," I said. "I know how to take care of myself. And don't worry about your job, I'll tell my brother it was my fault."

"You don't understand," he said.

"Don't come near me," I said. "If you come near me, you'll really lose the job," and walked away from him down the lane. The children under the guinep tree had seen the skirmish and they ran behind me chanting: "The boy can't fight, the boy can't fight. Him pants so tight and the boy can't fight."

Then a sound like firecrackers and the children fell to the ground. So did I. Bullets whizzed over our heads and the door to Verna's house slammed shut. Then silence. Feet scurrying away into the distance.

One of the children, a young boy, crawled over to my side.

"Look like smady want you dead, mister. Leave before them kill we too."

I took his advice and ran out into the lane, all the while looking over my shoulder, and headed towards the college.

The sun rose in the middle of the sky and John crows flew over the tops of the trees. Above the electric lines a kite, trapped in a mango tree, flapped in the wind. The smell of burning rubber crept through the lane.

Over the tops of the shanties, crackling sound frizzled the silence. The DJ put another record on the turntable, and the bass thundered over the zinc roofs.

"Here comes another pick from the past. Hope this one will really last. Here it comes with a flick of my wrist. This one will make ya really bounce and twist."

I turned the corner and made for my alma mater.

CHAPTER SEVEN

Jamaica College was a field of faded majesty. The road leading to the main office had fallen into disrepair and its speckled surface humped along between the charred embankments shrubbed with stiff weeds. I tore the red cloth off my arm and as I passed St. Dunstan's Chapel, I looked up at the inscription on the memorial: "In memory of the seventeen gallant gentlemen, sometime scholars, brothers-in-arms, who gave their lives in the Great War fighting for the freedom of the world. Lest we forget, 1914-1918." It had been smeared with graffiti.

Light filtering through the burglar bars on the west window – a replica of St. Dunstan's window in Canterbury Cathedral – dappled the altar and the candleholders that were welded to the font. The corridor where our young voices, unbroken by time, would climb up the rafters every Sunday with *Kyrie, Kyrie Eleison* was now submerged in shadows and the smell of rotting limes. I rubbed the dust off the window and then could almost feel the rush of prefects behind me. They had taunted and beaten me all through the lower and upper school, until Reuben showed up and taught me how to defend myself. Those I couldn't handle, he took care of for me.

I felt like gagging. Tony's punch had made a gash in the side of my mouth. I sprinted across "Holy Ground", a strip of land dedicated to the founder's conception of the school as an hermetically sealed garden. Towering above the quadrangle, gargoyles, their shields blackened by soot, stood guard over the deserted stables and drained swimming pool beside the dormitories.

A dry wind blew over the cricket patch stirring small whirlwinds of dust over the stalks of grass and wild calaloo, lifting them up to the fractured cornices above the Assembly Hall that opened onto the soccer field.

I loved playing soccer. It was a simple game. There was a ball and two opposing teams that wore different coloured jerseys. You had your team-mates and they had theirs. The position I played, striker, demanded a single-minded purpose: to put the ball in the back of the net. With a link man like Reuben, I'd take off running, without getting offside, and the ball would appear magically at my feet. All I had to do was *salad* a centre-half, pushing the ball through his legs and run around him. No one could beat our combination. It was just that simple.

But off the field everything was different. Nothing was certain. I didn't know who was on my side and people were changing their jerseys, back and forth, in the middle of the game. One minute they were on my side and the next minute they weren't. Whose side was I on now?

I stopped by a water cooler but the water had been locked off. I spat bloodied saliva on the azaleas beside the steps and hurried over to Scotland Hall where Doc was waiting inside the lab. I peeped inside the door and he looked up immediately.

"You're early" he said, "This is new. Maybe they taught you something useful in the States. Something we couldn't teach you here."

"How are you, Sir?" I said and glanced up at the clock on the wall behind him. It was eleven thirty-two.

A stickler for punctuality, Doc once said in a discussion we had in the Great Room that if we could get Jamaicans to obey the clock, then half of the island's problems would be solved. I told him that my fellow countrymen and I were merely viewing time in more creative manner. He told me to stop smoking weed.

"Very well," he said. Ash from his cigar fell on his khaki pants, and he dusted them with his handkerchief. "You'll have to wait until I finish this before we go to my office."

He stubbed his cigar and handed me a lab coat. What new mad experiment was he up to now?

Doc, our resident mad scientist and Renaissance man rolled up in one, had thrown himself into his work after Adele, his only child, ran off with an elder from the Twelve Tribes of Israel. After Adele left home, he became more opposed to the dreads and we suffered. He revived an old school rule against beards and moustaches, and vetoed our plans for changing the school uniform in the upper school from blazers to bush jackets.

If Doc was determined to rid Jamaica College of all Rasta influence, we fought him every step of the way. Rasta gave us pride, made us feel proud to be young Jamaicans. We could live without the sinking feeling of never measuring up to British standards – that always began and ended with colour, class, or religion – of what it meant to be civilized gentlemen. Or just human. And although Doc had abolished candle greasing and other traditions imported from the English public schools, in that difficult time, in our young revolutionary minds we thought he was the worst thing that could have happened to Jamaica College. Doc belonged to that small percentage of young Caribbean men who had gone off to England during the fifties who were convinced that because of the size of our economies, independence from England had not been the best strategy for the island's development. We disagreed and vowed to fight the collaborator all the way.

★★★

But there were other political currents in those days that were less easy for people like me to embrace. Into the old wars between Blacks and Browns entered the new rhetoric of Black Power. All whites were guilty of counter-revolutionary acts, and brown people, the mongrels and house slaves as they called us, were excluded and feared on both sides of the racial divide. No one knew for certain where our true allegiances lay – and how could they, we were all individuals, as contentious to the core as all our countrymen, black, brown or white. Our history teacher, Freeman Lightbourne (a short mousy man whose Afro and beard covered his face, so that looking at him without his glasses, all you saw was two black seeds peering out from a mass of black hair), would begin each class by haranguing Larry and me. When we got to the Apprenticeship period, he dropped his notes, peered out from his reading glasses, and said, "Emancipation was bitterly opposed by the plantocracy, so a compromise was reached with the former slave owners," and he looked dead at us.

Plantocracy. That was the word he loved and he'd use it whenever he called on us to answer a question. We had better sense than to actually talk in class, knowing he was looking for any chance to humiliate us.

"Mr. Buchanan of the famous Buchanan clan," he would say, calling on us when he thought we'd been silent for too long, "Great grandson of the Custos of St. Thomas, when did the Apprenticeship period end?"

"In 1838," Larry said tersely.

"Very good, Custos Buchanan," he said. "Say hello to the fellow members of the plantocracy."

His goading continued until near the end of the semester when Keith "Blacka" Samuels told Mr. Lightbourne to stop it. Blacka, the class bully who was already six feet tall in first form, got his name after a boy told him his mother was so black, they marked her absent at night school. Blacka beat the boy to a pulp.

Larry thanked Blacka, but said he could defend himself.

"You should give thanks, you poke-hearted bumbo claat, I taking up for you," Blacka said.

"I can stand up for myself," said Larry, "without any help from you. Thanks anyway."

Blacka was offended and before we knew it the two of them were outside. Blacka charged at Larry with a cricket bat and Larry dodged him. He came at Larry again and Larry dived beside a pile of wood and sheet metal and pulled out a two by four.

Larry blocked every blow, but never retaliated. Ten minutes into the brawl, when Blacka realized he wasn't getting anywhere – Larry was a purple belt in Tae-Kwon-Do from the time he was six – Blacka threw down the bat and said, "Fuck this shit. Next time, white boy."

When Larry was sure Blacka was gone, he dropped the piece of board. I was impressed with how he'd handled himself.

"You know he's going to try again. Why didn't you hit him so he wouldn't come back?" I asked.

"When he does, I'll be ready," he said. "But don't you think our ancestors have hit enough people in this country?"

★★★

At first, Doc was hired every spring semester to teach human sexuality to the fifth formers who were about to take the GCE exams. The full-time teacher, Phyllis McEwen, or as we called her Syphilis McUrine, refused to teach the course after a particularly nasty encounter with Larry that involved the female reproductive cycle.

When Larry found out that Doc was going to be teaching the course, he decided to test him, and he waited for the right moment. It came two weeks before Christmas when Doc said, "Upon ejaculation, the male..." Larry's hand shot up in the air. "How much sperm is ejaculated, Sir?" The class broke out in laughter, but Doc turned it around quickly, "How much do you think, Mr. Buchanan, given your recent experiments in the WC?" The class held its breath. Larry was not fazed. "About a gallon, Sir?" The class was almost

104

out of control. "My God," said Doc, "we are trying to impregnate, not drown." The class exploded. Doc had won.

I put on the lab coat and went with him inside the lab. The shelves were lined with cages with rats and bottles with dogfish, alligators, and a human foetus that had always disgusted and fascinated me. Sometimes I would walk inside the lab, ostensibly to ask Doc a question, but really to peek at the leathery comma inside the jar. It seemed so human – fingers, toes, with its eyes closed, almost alive – yet remarkably preserved in its formaldehyde bath. Each generation of schoolboys had invented their own history for the foetus, but all seemed convinced it was one of Doc's experiments gone awry.

Yet despite the general mockery, there were boys who aped his mannerisms and his Oxbridge accent. Doc may have been wrong about many things, but he was brilliant, and for those young boys that was the one quality they respected.

"I'll be finished in a second," said Doc. He sat down in front of a table with a shuttle box that had wires running in and out of the back. Although the Bunsen burners had been turned off, I could still detect a faint odour of gas in the lab. He flicked open a pad, pulled out his pen and set the timer on his watch.

"Take your time," I said. I was lying, but I knew he didn't like to be rushed, and if he sensed any urgency on my part, he would delay. "I'm in no hurry. Besides, it looks interesting. What are you working on?"

"Pavlovian conditioning," he said, his eyes brightening. "What I'm doing is setting up a control group over here. The defining characteristic of my experiment is to give these rats here," pointing to the shuttle box, "inescapable shocks where no voluntary response from the animal will influence the severity or the duration of the shocks. The shocks are uncontrollable. The timing, length, and intensity are determined only by me."

I took a chance. "Still playing God, I see."

He continued as if I hadn't said anything.

"I'm writing a paper with my colleagues at the university." He scribbled something on the pad. "It's going to be called learned helplessness as social metastasis or something like that. I'll have the students dream up a sexy title so it will be published."

"What are you trying to prove?" I asked, feigning interest so he would hurry up.

"It's really a development on the theories of Martin Seligman," he said with an air of indifference. "The distinctive aspect of my experiment is I'm using rats from Standpipe. My Group 3. We began with a group of healthy rats and switched the electrical shock from the left side of the cage to the right side of the cage and then the entire floor of the cage. Then we opened the door and instead of scurrying out, they just stayed there and took the shocks. They had given up hope. But I'm taking it one step further. I'm going to prove that if you introduce rats that have learned helplessness as a result of the shocks – Group 2 – into a healthy community – Group 1 – then the control group, over time, will begin to show the same pathological behaviours as Group 2. These effects will be seen long after the infected rats have been removed from the control group."

"And where do the Standpipe rats come in?"

"The standard wild rats, *Rattus norwegus*, resist with alarming ferocity any attempt to capture them. That's why, once we have shocked them into submission, their subsequent helplessness is the more astonishing."

Doc pressed the lever that delivered shocks to the rats and timed the duration. The rat scurried around the cage unable to escape. Doc noted the time then wrote on his pad.

"But what's more interesting," he said as he paused for fifteen seconds, "is the behaviour of the Standpipe rats once they are introduced into the control group. And by the way," he guffawed, "I think Standpipe's rats should be given their own category *Rattus Standpipus*. If they fight with the other rats, as they almost invariably do, they retain normal levels of norephrinine, the hormone that controls depression and general emotional health in rats – and in the college sophomores that we've tested. By fighting, they stave off the myriad forms of depression and suicidal tendencies."

"The rats or the sophomores?" I asked.

"Both," he said, unfazed by my comment. "It may be a case of putting the cart before the horse, but these rats here, the warriors, while chewing on their neighbours' skulls, are actually keeping their emotional health intact."

"So fighting is a means of resisting depression?"

I could feel a bloody lump on my tongue.

"Yes," he said gleefully, "and these Standpipe rats, do they fight or do they fight!" The buzzer on his watch went off again and he pressed the lever. "I was thinking of including some graphic pictures of a particularly bloody encounter, but what would be the point? But come with me, I'm finished here."

He raised his hand off the lever and wrote on the pad. He got up from the table and took off the lab coat. I handed him my lab coat and we walked down the hallway to his office.

"You seemed surprised back there," he said. "Don't be. That's a reflection of the natural world, how things really are. We protected you within these walls so when we sent you out into the Standpipes of the world, you would be our standard bearer, a brave soldier against the forces of entropy."

Good old Doc. Always the warrior. Always out there marching to the tune of "Onward Christian Soldiers", but with secular lyrics. He had trained us to take up the battle, so when the old warrior, God forbid, could no longer raise his lance, some young squire would step into the fray and display the colours that would drive fear into the heart of man or beast. "Work is burning in the fields," was his battle cry. And he had the nerve to call me idealistic.

Down the hallway, while Doc was relighting his cigar, I saw one of the groundsmen setting up a table with a pitcher of water. I was about to turn back when Doc said, "Don't delay, I have a box seat at Sabina waiting for me. Let's get this over with as quickly as possible. Your father always wanted you to have this. Too bad he died before you could collect it."

"Why did he want me to have it, it's just metal and wood."

"It's more than that," he said. "You of all people know better than that. No other father and son won so many athletic awards in the history of the college. Your father wanted you to collect it."

"Is that why you've kept it here, why you never allowed Chris to pick it up for me?"

"Chris would never appreciate the value of this award. He breezed through Jamaica College without learning the traditions that are rooted in here. That's why he got into trouble."

"He was always high-spirited, Sir. He beat up that prefect because he wouldn't be humiliated by anyone."

"The prefects kept order in the school," said Doc, jabbing his stubby index finger in the air.

Doc believed in the prefect system because he felt it prepared us to handle power in the future. A prefect was a student in the upper school who had all the authority of a teacher, with the exception of the power to cane. But who needed caning when you could force a boy to stand for hours with a jock strap over his head, cock rockets they called it, order him to write lines such as, "Persistent perversity provokes the patient pedagogue producing particularly painful punishment," a thousand times, or any other kind of public humiliation. Once I became a prefect I ended all of these abuses, but didn't have the time to completely eradicate them from JC. Two years after I left, everything that I'd worked for was reversed.

"But what kind of order? They were brutal. A prefect, if he didn't like you, had the power to force you to do anything under the pretext of order. If you forgot to wear your tie at breakfast, he could order you to wash his jock strap."

"But you don't attack a prefect in the way Chris did," said

Doc. "He beat that boy senseless over a mere trifle. He almost killed that boy, and for what? For sullying his shoes! No, if you want real change, you do as you eventually did. You work your way through the system, become a prefect, and then change the system. But then again, not everyone thinks about wrong and right as you do. You worked harder than anyone to change the rules."

"Sir, I had two years to change over a hundred years of school tradition. And I remember you once called me an idealist and a radical."

"That was because you wanted to change the school flag."

"Sir, it had the Union Jack in the corner! Sir, we had to resist their rule."

"But was it worth getting rid of something so small, to expend so much energy on something so insignificant to bring about the change you wanted?"

"Sir, it meant everything. We couldn't keep bowing to the British."

But Doc would never understand. He'd bought the whole English tradition lock, stock and barrel. I, too, had inherited that tradition. The very tools I used to criticize were tainted by that tradition. How could I separate the valuable from the dross in a tradition that had insisted on my subservience, and treated me as less than human while expecting me to carry on its ideals? Ideals that seemed noble, but were founded on inhumanity and exclusion. What remained after the winnowing? But whether I liked it or not, the values *were* a part of me, made me who I was, for better or worse.

Pulling the keys from his pocket, Doc opened the door and went straight to his desk. The office walls were covered with portraits of former headmasters and Old Boys. I recognized the face of a former Old Boy who, we later learned, after our graduating class greeted him with boos, was one of the framers of the Jamaican Constitution. Doc would trot him out in a wheelchair at every graduation and he would stand for the National Anthem, then wave to us before they carted him back to a nursing home where he'd wait for the next graduation.

Doc searched all the drawers in his desk and I peered through the window that offered a clear view to the tuck shop. So that's how he saw us, I now realized, when we used to sneak into Standpipe to buy cigarettes. And then I saw Tony hiding behind the woodwork shop. Why was he still following me?

Doc looked at me with a look of blank puzzlement. "It isn't here," he said. "I'm certain it was here this morning."

"I'm sure you've just misplaced it," I said. I was relieved that I wouldn't be dragging that thing around for the rest of the day.

"I don't misplace anything," he said. "I left that plaque in my desk right here this morning!"

When he realized he had snapped at me, he said, "I'm sorry, Jason. It's that I've had an odd feeling since last night when the night watchman told me he'd seen that psychotic on the campus."

"Which one? The island is filled with psychotics."

"The king of all psychotics," said Doc. "Papa Legba or whatever he calls himself these days. I don't know what the connection is, but I can bet you he's tied in with this somehow."

"Are you sure? What would he have to do with this?"

"He's the only one who could have done this," he said. "He's the only one who can intimidate the groundsmen and people in general with his mumbo jumbo. He gets in and out of places because everyone's afraid of him."

"I'm not afraid of him."

"Well, you should be," he said. "Only you and your father, it seems, weren't afraid of him. Your father defended him on murder charges a few years ago."

"Murder? Papa Legba wouldn't harm a soul," I said.

"Maybe not a soul, but he is, I'm sure, capable of murder. The dead man had been accused of molesting children and because the children wouldn't testify against him, and because he was one of these so-called rankings, the court released him. Papa Legba's dogs almost led the police to the body on the land he claims is his, which, by the way, your father secured for him under the provision of squatter's rights. Your father always took the matter of defending," he paused, "pardon the pun, the underdogs, a bit too far, I thought. The police charged Papa Legba with murder and he would have gone to the gallows if your father hadn't intervened. I, for one, am convinced he did it. He's capable of anything."

A part of me was inclined to believe Doc. If a child was involved, I could see Papa Legba punishing the man in any way he saw fit. But would he go so far as to take a life? To lead a blow against Babylon?

I moved the chair closer to the window so I could pay attention to Doc and watch the front door of the tuck shop.

"Carmichael was all for sending him off to jail, and as far as I was concerned, it would have been good riddance."

"But what would he want with the plaque?"

"Your guess is as good as mine. The man is certifiably insane from smoking all that marijuana – he's like your old art teacher Basil Cunningham. That's another one they should put away and will. His ego is too big for this island. "

"What do you mean?"

"I'm afraid that it's his pen rather than his penis that has gotten him into trouble," and he chuckled, pleased at his pun. "He may be fired this fall from the college."

"But why? What has he done?"

"He wrote an article in *The Gleaner* calling for the legalization of marijuana. At the time, our government was negotiating with Washington for increased aid. His article couldn't have come at a worse time. He had to be denounced in the firmest measures."

"And you, of course, helped."

"Oh no, I stayed out of that one."

Doc and Basil had never gotten along. When Basil came back from the States and tried to get a job at Jamaica College, Doc tried to block him. From what Dada once told me, the only reason Basil was hired was because he was an Old Boy

111

and called in a few favours. Doc blasted him as a "Neo-Negro Philist" and Basil answered in *The Gleaner* by calling Doc an "Afro-Saxon". Basil was always fond of extending their arguments in the press. On Sundays I'd take *The Gleaner* out on the verandah of the dorm and curl up in the Adirondack chairs and try to figure out who had won that week.

"He has been, I am told, totally discredited. He won't be receiving any more commissions from the government to produce his so-called paintings."

"But he's one of the island's best artists! He's won so many awards. Guggenheims in America..."

"Americans," snorted Doc, "what do they know about art? Like Romans they know how to build roads, but art?" He kissed his teeth. "Their civilization, if one may call it that, has managed to perpetrate the biggest frauds in history. They have corrupted every standard of taste and civility in the name of commerce. Their relentless pursuit of novelty uproots all the traditions of good taste and has debased all of us while attempting to remake the world in their image."

It was no use arguing with him on this point. It would be the same discussion that we'd had so many times when I graduated to sixth form and debated with him the pros and cons of every issue – many times for the hell of it.

For Doc to consider that Basil's break with representational art enabled him to make a direct aesthetic statement he couldn't make in any other way, would be akin to asking Margaret Thatcher to accept the equality of all Commonwealth citizens in Britain – native born or not.

"Sir, you're absolutely right about the Americans," I said. "But I would argue that Basil is merely trying to get us to face aspects of our past that we still haven't accepted." It was useless, but I had to defend my friend.

"But where is this pied piper leading us? A future that worships destruction, anarchy? Look what their revolution has brought us. They've shown us the past, but they've unleashed demons that make our future nasty, brutish and short."

"But does Basil deserve all the blame?"

"He was the leader of the barbarians who overturned everything. With his friends who wrote plays without plots, poets who had no sense of line, tropes that never reached above the navel, and whose only theme, if they had one, was of alienation and class warfare, or his own paintings that were circles, scribbles and broken lines. They all created misery. One never sensed in their work *joie de vivre*."

Doc straightened his head and held his back as straight as a ramrod. The muscles in his neck tightened and his forehead was furrowed with wrinkles.

"They are," he said with an air of superiority, "guilty of pride and arrogance caused by the seduction of technology."

This at least was new, I thought. "The seduction of technology?"

His eyes brightened. He knew he had me. "We are," he paused, "no different than those rutting *Homo sapiens* who daubed their images in the caves at Lascaux. But because we, in this century, found methods to channel electricity and made some amazing technological advances, we have been seduced into thinking that our century is somehow different, that the species has changed."

"Haven't we?" I said. "We've advanced to the point where we no longer have slavery, and women aren't viewed as second-class citizens."

I said the part about women as a dig at him, because Doc had also blocked an attempt by Carmichael to make Jamaica College into a co-ed school. All the Old Boys, except me, stood behind Doc in opposing Carmichael.

"Sir," I had said, pleading in front of the Student Council, "there will come a day when we will leave this school and we had better know how to live with women and treat them with respect and not as something, something other. If we really believe in the ideals of this school, then we better say everyone can play the game, regardless of sex."

I knew it was going to be a tough battle, so I went to Papa Legba to tell him about it, and he agreed with Doc. This was the one part of his theology that baffled me. It was totally inconsistent with his idea of oneness.

"The glory of a man is his wisdom and overstanding, and the glory of woman is in her king-man."

When he said that, I knew the measure wouldn't pass.

Doc cleared his throat. "But we have the perennial problem of evil," he said. "Or in your new philosophy, have you forgotten about the Holocaust in Europe? The animal hasn't changed. The noble purpose of art, especially in the West, is to remind us of our identity. And we are Western, and not African as Cunningham seems to believe. Only art from the Western tradition can tell us who we really are."

"And where we've been, and where we're going?"

"We're all going to Standpipe."

I looked through the window at the cricket pitch. A wisp of smoke, caught by the wind, drifted through the window. I searched the campus for some patch of green, but couldn't find any. I was relieved Nicole had left. I had bragged to her so much about this place and now it had fallen to moss, stone and vine.

The sun burned through the fronds of the royal palms and dust swirled around the drained swimming pool. Pools of stagnant water with almond leaves and mosquito larvae choked the gutters around the patio of the cafeteria. Behind the cafeteria, lime trees bent their blighted leaves against the tiled roof of the metal workshop where I had made an ashtray for my mother at Christmas.

★★★

I was thirteen and it was the first time I was going to visit my mother, Myriam, since I'd entered Jamaica College. I'd been looking forward to seeing her ever since she sent the plane tickets in late November. I worked on the ashtray for the rest of the semester. My mother didn't smoke, but it was the only thing I could make. While other boys were making test tube racks in woodwork or elaborate candleholders in metal work, all I could do was beat out a piece of tin with raised sides and an indentation in the middle. But it did have some intricate designs that I'd etched all around the sides and in the indentations where the cigarettes would have been placed.

When she picked me up at the airport, I could hardly wait to show her. And I could tell she was excited. She told me how happy she was and that she'd finally found "The Truth". She said she'd left the Seventh Day Adventists and was now a Jehovah's Witness. At that time I didn't know who they were, so I went along with her, happy that she was happy. She told me about her plans to enroll me in Bible classes and that I'd start going to the Kingdom Hall. She said we would go door to door and that we would have a wonderful time witnessing. I didn't say anything. I was bristling with pride. I couldn't wait to get home to give her the Christmas present.

When we got home, she showed me my room and where to put my things. I couldn't wait any longer. I told her to go to her room and as soon as she left, I dug through my soccer shorts and found the ashtray wrapped in a pair of socks.

"I hope you aren't peeking," I said.

"No," she said.

When I went in the room, she was sitting on her bed with her back to the door. I held the ashtray behind my back and told her to turn around. As she turned around I screamed, "Merry Christmas!"

A look of horror covered her face. She grabbed the ashtray out of my hand and ran to the kitchen. She crushed the ashtray and threw it in the garbage can.

"Never say those words in this house! Don't you know that it's a pagan holiday converted by the Roman Catholic Church?"

"I didn't know," I said. "I made it for you."

"I don't smoke and I don't allow smoking in my house," she said. "Now come over here and give me a hug. We're going to have to start your re-education right away. I don't know what Albert has been teaching you, but you better forget all that he's told you. It's all lies. Don't listen to him."

I gave her a hug and looked down at the ashtray in the garbage can. I loved my mother. It was worth the sacrifice.

★★★

The bloody aftertaste spread over my mouth. Tony's punch had injured me worse than I thought.

My tongue was heavy and leaden and it was becoming difficult to swallow. I needed to get some water.

"I must be going now," I said, and glanced through the window again. Still no sign of Adrian, but Tony was still around.

"I'm really sorry," said Doc, "you came all this way for what appears to be a futile effort."

"It's okay," I said and got up from my chair. Doc rose and shook my hand. I walked back with him to the front of building. The groundsman, covered with grass clippings was shaking his transistor radio. The batteries were going dead. He had finished setting up the table with a tumbler of water with ice and paper cups. I went over to the table and Doc followed me. Doc tapped him on the shoulder.

"How many wickets have we lost?" Doc asked.

"Ninety-five for the loss of one," said the groundsman without turning around.

When he realized it was Doc, he straightened up and tightened the cord around his waist that kept his belly from pouring over the front of his pants.

"You hear the news, sah? The police say them find out who is the other somebody who kill Mr. Lumley. Them say him used to come here, sah."

"Impossible," said Doc. "What was his name?"

"Is true, sah. Them say him name Adrian Matthews."

"Can't say I recall him," said Doc.

"I do," I said trying to hide my amazement. "He was the boy who was expelled for defacing my father's plaque."

116

"Ah, yes," said Doc, "how could I have forgotten. It doesn't surprise me. He was a Standpipe boy. Another one of your father's failed efforts. Trying to help the poor bastards. Nothing good ever comes out of there. It really hurt him that someone whom he was trying to help would have betrayed him like that. Your father pushed for his expulsion. Later, if I remember correctly, you tried to stand up for him, but it didn't work."

"Yes, I did. But I didn't try hard enough."

Doc didn't say anything. He shook my hand again and went back to the lab. He put on his lab coat and wiped his hands with alcohol before sitting in front of the shuttle box. I knew now I had to see Basil. I left Doc alone in the lab and walked out to the front Scotland Hall. The groundsman looked around, spat and went back to listening to a news report about a drowned man off Hellshire Beach.

CHAPTER EIGHT

"And they're off and running." The tipsters and the touters had gathered outside Watson's Off Course Betting for the third race. Crouched, as if riding their favourites, they snapped their fingers and loosened the reins on their imaginary steeds.

Beside the store, a line snaked around a theatre for the latest Kung Fu flick, *The Drunken Warlord Meets the Shadow Master*. Boys from New Standpipe played in the street practising the moves they had seen on the screen: catapulting their thin bodies in the air, somersaulting, and landing feet first on the pavement.

I'd bought some patties at Tastee Patties and thought that if Nicole had been with me, this was one of the places I'd have taken her. Tastee Patties wasn't fancy, but they served the flakiest, most flavourful patties in Kingston. I bit into one. The hot sauce stung a bit now. I slurped down a cane juice and was on my way again.

I'd lost Tony in Cross Roads when I made a neat feint, pretending to board a minibus going to Half Way Tree and he'd jumped on the one behind and by the time he'd noticed I'd jumped off, his bus was on its way and wouldn't stop. I waved at him as his bus went by and I could see him arguing with the driver. So much for being soft!

As I eased through the crowd at the bus stop and across the front of a gas station, I was grabbed by a crippled woman on a cardboard boat, her useless legs doubled under her dress.

"Dunzai, dunzai for food," she begged. I struggled with her, but she wouldn't let me go.

"Dunzai for food. Dunzai for food." Her face was streaked with tar and oil and she made a smacking sound with her lips.

"Christ, let go of my leg," I pleaded, and I threw some coins on the ground and ran in the opposite direction.

I crossed to the other side of the avenue, away from the minibus station and entered a complex of town houses surrounded by mango trees of every kind: Julie, Bombay, and my favourite, East Indian. The trees were in season and their blackened limbs hung heavy with fruit.

The parking lot in front of the townhouses was deserted and as I approached Basil's front door, the sweet smell of resinous herb seeped under the doorway and greeted me in the small garden at the front of his apartment. I knocked at the door but there was no answer. I stepped back, went through the gate, and walked around to the parking lot. Basil's VW van was parked under a banyan, so I knew he was home.

"Jason! I thought I recognized you." His voice caught me off-guard and I looked up. Basil was standing by the upstairs window. He wasn't wearing his eye-patch. "Come up! I've opened the door."

I walked into Basil's living room. It had been converted into a studio and was separated from the rest of the house by slabs of plywood barely held in place by wooden slats nailed to the floor. The slabs rocked uneasily on the nails and looked as if they had been bent back and forth by someone trying to wrench them from their base. The walls of the living room were cratered with holes gouged by a battering ram or a crow bar. In the middle of the studio were a blank canvas and a pile of newspapers covered with a drape. A workbench spattered with dried paint faced a rocking chair by the window.

"You cost me a good spliff," he said as he came towards

me. He was in his work clothes: denim overalls and a long-sleeved shirt, but he still had the towel wrapped around his neck. He locked the door behind me and said, "I flushed the spliff down the toilet when I heard the knock on the door. I thought you were the police."

He hugged me, then backed away. "Shit, what happened to you?"

"Some mad woman grabbed me on the way here."

"Myrtle," he said. "She hit you? Your face is swollen."

"You know her?"

"Know her, she's a fixture around here, but she only hurts herself. She used to be a preacher man's wife until she ran off with a taxi man from Bull Bay. But let me get some ice for your face. Go upstairs and wash yourself. The bathroom is still upstairs to your left."

"You have water?"

"This is New Standpipe," he said. "We have everything because the American Consulate is right down the road."

In the bathroom I looked into the mirror. The gash in my mouth was open. My back teeth were bloodstained and my right cheek was slightly swollen, but it wasn't as bad as Basil made it sound. I tried to get a better angle to examine the gash, but the mirror was cracked and some of the silvering was missing. I turned on the tap and rinsed out my mouth.

Basil met me as I was coming down the stairs. He balanced two drinks in his left hand and handed me a rag and a bowl of ice.

"Here, drink this," he said. "It's the only other anaesthetic I have."

I wrapped some ice in the rag and held it to my cheek. I sat on the workbench and Basil on his rocking chair.

"So why did Myrtle hit you? She's never hit anyone."

"She didn't hit me," I said. "This was the work of Tony, my driver."

"What did you do?"

"I don't know."

"Jason, you must have said or done something to upset him."

"It may have been because I said something about us being related. I don't know."

"And he hit you for that? There must be more."

Basil leaned forward in the chair and cupped his drink in his hand.

"When his mother left, one of the maids told me my stepmother had sent her way because she suspected my father was sleeping with her."

"Exercising the old slave master's prerogative, eh?"

"I guess so. Though in some cases it mightn't have been anything like that."

"What are you saying?" The ice crackled in Basil's glass. "Do you think that it could have been anything but harassment? You old romantic. Think about it, Jason. Think about how the women felt when they knew their job depended on sleeping with the busha. Black, brown, or white."

He moved the towel from around his neck and cleaned the soap from behind his ears and his throat.

"Christ, this hurts," I said.

"You'll get over it," said Basil. "Keep that rag on your face. So where is he now? I didn't see him drive up."

"I left him at Jamaica College…"

"You were in Standpipe?" said Basil in disbelief. "You're brave."

"I think I was shot at…"

"I'm not surprised. Don't take it personally, you're lucky you weren't killed."

"I take everything personally, even the way the college looks. It, it looks like a dump heap. I'm almost ashamed to say I went there."

"I wouldn't know," said Basil, "I haven't been there in a long time."

"I heard. Doc told me."

"What did he tell you?" Basil inquired. "I can bet he was happy to see me being forced out."

"He didn't tell me anything, but he was practically beaming when he told me that you might be leaving."

"That old fucker," said Basil. "He's one of those who've been pushing to get rid of me. But what were you doing there?"

"It's a long story, Basil."

"We have all afternoon," he said. "I've finished working so I have the rest of the day off. Cheers," and we clinked our glasses together.

I waited before I took another sip. The nerves in my jaw spread a web of pain across my cheeks.

"Okay, I went to JC this morning supposedly to collect a plaque that the Old Boys had given to my father and me. Some father and son achievement in track and field, but I was really there to see an old friend of mine, who I've now learned from the radio had something to do with my father's death, but I don't believe the report."

"What's his name?"

"Haven't you been following the cricket..." I stopped. Sports never interested Basil. For Basil to even consider attending a cricket match was like asking Peter Tosh to open Parliament in Britain – without a bomb. "His name's Adrian Matthews," I said.

"Can't place the name, but this is interesting. That's the second time you've said my father. That's a change. What's come over you, a sudden nostalgia? Since when have you referred to Albert as your father?"

"Since I learned this morning that he could be my father."

"There were rumours," he said.

"This isn't rumour," I said and showed him the paper that I had folded into my wallet. As he read it I said, "What I can't understand is why no-one, including you of all people, ever told me."

Basil handed me the paper and I put it back into my wallet. He leaned back in the rocking chair and looked through the window.

"Let me ask you," he said. "Would you have listened to

anyone, me included, if I came to you with a story like that? You're the one who went through Jamaica College as Jason Stewart. You were so caught up in yourself. Suppose I had come up to you with that rumour, what would you have done?"

"Hated you," I confessed. "I'd have never listened to you again."

"So why should I have risked our friendship on something that only your father and your mother knew for sure?"

"And they're both dead, so I'll never know."

"Paternity is a myth anyway," said Basil. "Men can only be comrades. But I still don't understand why you'd go into Standpipe to meet this thug."

"Because he asked me," I said. "And he's not a thug, he's my friend."

"You don't always give in because someone asks you," said Basil slyly.

I hesitated. I didn't want to tell him, but he was the only one who had defended me when I moved out of my father's house. I put the ice-filled rag on the floor; my cheek was becoming numb.

"I was meeting him because I believe whatever trouble he's gotten himself into, it's my fault. I'm the one to blame for all this."

"You've lost me," said Basil.

"No one knows this. I've never told you before, but I'm the reason why Adrian got expelled from Jamaica College."

"Now I know!" said Basil, his eyes suddenly coming alive. "He's the Standpipe boy. Came to us late. In fifth form."

"Yes, but he only stayed a year. He was a bit older than the rest of us so he had a hard time fitting in. He and I became friends when we realized that we both knew Papa Legba."

"Your infamous Rasta days," said Basil. "We were all worried about you, that you'd become Rasta. When you were wandering around with that character who looks like an extra in a bad Cecil B. De Mille movie. Back then, you were smoking so much weed, I'd watch you both totter into the dorms. Rasta seemed the next logical step. Young rich boy meets ghetto youth, friendship develops, joins Rasta. It was pretty clichéd."

"But I didn't join," I said. "But Rasta made me realize many things. Although I could never accept Haile Selassie as the reincarnated Christ, it helped me overcome my woundedness over my wealth, my colour, and my class. I saw the oneness in things – like the light the Impressionists said suffused all things. You taught us that."

"I taught you boys a lot of crap..."

"Well, through Rasta, Adrian and I became idrens. We went through a lot together. For one thing he put an end to the prefects' torments."

"That would have stopped if you'd used your real name, if you'd told everyone who your father was. You brought that one on yourself."

"Either way it stopped. He beat up a prefect who'd made me wear a chamber pot over my head."

"Crowning," said Basil. "The one, the only good thing, that Doc and I ever agreed about. We abolished it in his first week as principal."

"None of the prefects ever bothered me again, and when we both made the soccer team, and the other teams would poke me in the eye or elbow me, he was my enforcer. Then, he taught me how to fight back. How to throw an elbow without the ref seeing. I never thought that two people from such different backgrounds could be so close."

"I think I know where this is heading," said Basil.

"Get your mind out of the gutter," I said.

"One man's gutter is another man's heaven," he countered.

I could never match wits with Basil, but I needed to tell someone. When I left the island this time, I wouldn't be leaving any ghosts behind. I took another sip of my drink.

"One afternoon, after soccer training, we were coming down the road from the barracks when we saw that the trophy room was open. We went inside and saw all the trophies, soccer gear, T-shirts, socks, old footballs. The inner room had all the trophies and plaques. Adrian decided to liberate a few T-shirts and while he was stuffing them into his bag, I walked back into the trophy room and scrawled..."

"Cocksucker!" said Basil emphatically. 'That's how your father was brought in. He's the one who got Adrian expelled. He's the one who should be blamed, if anything. He's the one who pressed charges when it could have been treated solely as a school matter."

"But I was the one who talked Adrian into going into the store room. I knew the plaque was there. I had the chance and I took it. I scrawled that word and he took the blame. When the prefects caught him coming out of the storeroom with the socks and T-shirts, they held him and they called the police. He didn't say a thing. When they took him over to the main building, I was hiding behind the lockers. I waited until I thought everyone was gone and sneaked through the window. Throughout it all he didn't say anything."

"He had a choice all the while," said Basil. He leaned forward and buttoned the cuffs of his shirt.

"Yes, he did," I said, "but he didn't squeal. He was expelled for something I did. His one chance to make a better life and I blew it for him."

"Don't blame yourself for everything; it might have worked out for the best."

"I thought everything had worked out for the best. He left before everything was over. Papa Legba told me he'd gone to England to play soccer and was doing well."

"So what happened?"

"I don't know," I said. "When I moved to Miami, I lost contact with everyone. But from what I could understand yesterday, when I talked with him on the phone, he had some kind of knee injury and had to come back. But I still can't understand how he would be involved in my father's death. Do you think he could do it?"

"I don't know. It is possible. If he came back to Stand-pipe," said Basil wearily, "especially with a record, there's not much he could do. The gangs and crack are eating up Standpipe, the whole country. It's changing everything. The politicians who used to control the political gangs are only minimally in charge. Crack is cutting across all the political lines. The old boundaries of party and gangs are gone. But I shouldn't say anything. That's what got me into trouble in the first place."

Basil leaned back, put his arms over his head and yawned, stretching his limbs like an old tomcat, his white teeth showing through his moustache and goatee.

The light of the afternoon sun fell across Basil's shoulders. The sprinkler system for the complex's gardens sprayed a fine mist through the window, breaking the thin filaments that a spider had been deftly laying across the jalousies. The spider retreated to a corner to ponder its next move. Basil closed the window. Music from an adjoining townhouse throbbed against the wall.

"What kind of trouble have you gotten yourself into now?"

"It's nothing to joke about," he said. It was the first time I'd ever seen Basil worried about anything. "I may lose my job at Jamaica College."

"But why?"

"Me and my big mouth," he said wistfully. "A friend of mine was arrested for possession of herb and they were going to put him in prison. He was getting the herb for a mutual friend who's in the government. I tried the diplomatic way and when that didn't work, I wrote letters to *The Gleaner* and argued that we shouldn't be arresting poor men, some of them with families, for possession of herb. I suggested that the government would do better to arrest crack dealers and the big boys who were exporting the stuff by the bales, rather than arresting a poor man for a spliff."

"So what did they do?"

"They came here, and, of course, found some herb. They

didn't arrest me, but it was to show me that I had been warned. Your father led the charge against me. He ordered the arrest of several people within his own party – some fled to Miami to escape. He signed papers requesting their extradition."

He got up and walked around the room, showing me the damage the police had done to his studio and his paintings.

"Yeah, Dada hated the herb. I guess that's why I smoked so much at Jamaica College, so he would know. So it would hurt him. What I never could understand was that he would rail against me, and then he would defend Papa Legba if he got into trouble."

"Carmichael called him on that too. But your father said that was clearly for a religious use. He said he was against any other use. And he was ruthless, especially with the opposition. One of their junior senators accused your brother of being involved with drugs, but it was so preposterous that Carmichael forced him to issue a public apology. Everyone knew it was election year politics and political revenge."

"My brother will have his own revenge," I said. "I think he's going to run for my father's seat. His campaign strategy is to tie Carmichael to my father's death."

"Sounds like a good strategy to me. Son avenges father's death with campaign victory. And with his ambition, he could be the Prime Minister in the next couple of years."

"But you don't think Carmichael did it, do you?"

"Who knows? They're all armed to the teeth. The CIA supported your father's people with guns. They have all the guns, and the rest of us live behind burglar bars. What I'd like to know is where's Chris going to get the money? Everyone knows that your father left all his money to Emma. You guys are going to have to wait until she's dead to inherit."

Even though he was dead, my father had found another way to complicate my life. But this time the stakes were higher.

"I don't want any of his inheritance. Like Papa Legba

always says, 'Don't take no dead left.' No, my brother is going to use the money he's getting from the guesthouse. He looks as if he's doing pretty well."

I would keep some of my pride in front of Basil.

"That place? How on earth could he be making any money with it? I know it's on the beach, but it's too far out of the way. There's still no road, to speak of, to get there. I know the place. As an art gallery it didn't need to be easily accessible. In fact, that was part of its charm. Emma only needed to attract a few wealthy customers and we would eat for the next three months. But as a hotel, it's too deserted for him to be making any money on that place."

"But he is," I said. "He was offering packages to businesses in Miami for holiday retreats. He even offered me a honeymoon package. Maybe I should have taken it. Maybe I would have still have been married."

"I was sorry to hear about it," said Basil. "What caused you guys to split? You sounded so happy."

"I was. It was when we got married, we began moving in opposite directions. When I dropped out of college and lost my job as the assistant soccer coach that didn't help either. I refused any help from her parents and when the bills started coming in, the arguments started. She looked for comfort outside our bed, and the rest, as they say, is history."

"So how did your mother feel about it?"

"She was opposed to divorce, full stop. But she was the happiest woman alive when I got mine. She hated Simone and said I was weak, to begin with, to have married a girl like that."

"A girl like that?"

"My mother thought that I was still a virgin when I married Simone. And she'd done some checking up on her through her nurse friends, the Jackson Memorial Mafia. They told her all about her, family history and everything. But can we drop this," I said. "I've met someone else. She came down with me for the funeral."

"What's her name?"

"Nicole."

"She sounds perfect already," said Basil. "Only people with aspirations for upward mobility name their children Nicole, Ashley or Megan. So when do I meet her?"

"I don't know if you ever will. We keep having these arguments, you know."

"About what?"

Basil searched in his overalls for his cigarettes and matches. He fingered through his pockets, but couldn't find any.

"I think she wants me to quit my job."

"And what have you been doing with yourself?"

"Marketing." Then I stopped. I wouldn't lie any more. "I'm a telemarketer."

"You mean one of those guys that rip off senior citizens and scam old people out of their pensions and social security checks?"

"I never did that. Even when I was broke, without a penny, like a dog on the streets of Miami, I never did anything like that. I was still Myriam's son."

He found his Craven As, but the book of matches was empty. Dada used to say anyone who smoked Craven A could smoke ganja. Basil looked under the rags and found another book, but it was damp. Frustrated, he got up and went into the kitchen. He came back with a lit cigarette.

"I'll have one," I said.

Basil was shocked. "When did you start smoking again? I thought you'd stopped when you went to live with your mother?"

"I restarted somewhere between my divorce and my mother's death. When I lived with her I couldn't smoke; it was wicked, sinful, you know. But I didn't mind because I was happy to be around her after all those years. But let me tell you, divorce American style can bring out a lot of your vices and ones you didn't think you had. I don't smoke as much now, only when I'm nervous and drink this stuff."

I lit the cigarette and blew the smoke away. "Thank God it was in Florida, so I didn't have to pay alimony."

"But everything's settled, right?"

"Yeah, everything's settled, legally. She married my best friend from college who'd been screwing her behind my back."

"Sounds nasty," said Basil. "So how did you find out?"

"He gave her herpes. So she thought that she should tell me, so I could alert my doctor."

"That was awfully nice of her."

"It was, but I won't bore you with any more details. All I can tell you is that I went crazy. After the divorce I started drinking and doing crazy things like going to the apartment where they had their trysts. I had the landlord take me into the kitchen, living room, and bedroom. I sat on the bed and gazed through the window where they, no doubt, had lain and looked at the same tree, the same... I almost kill..."

Basil looked uncomfortable. But what he was hearing was no more than the quick spurt of pain from an old injury that runs up your spine and darts across your face – which leaves everyone thinking that you have some deep psychiatric problem.

"What made you stop?"

"My mother fell ill. I had to turn away from my own grief to take care of her. That's when I met Nicole. She helped me to take care of my mother's estate and saved me some money on taxes too. She also saved me from going under. I don't know what I would have done without her by my side. She's been my conscience when I thought I'd lost everything. But enough of me. What are you going to do if you lose your job?"

"I don't know what I'll do," he said. "I can't afford to lose my job. I can't afford to lose my health benefits with the school. But it all looks pretty bleak."

The sprinkler stopped and Basil opened the window. The gully behind the townhouses swallowed the shacks. Afternoon fires were being lit and the sulfur-yellow flames licked the sides of the fences. The smoke, like black incense, settled between the hills and the roofs glowed with the orange light from the setting sun. The crippled woman's wail shot through the eaves, "Dunzai, dunzai for food."

"But worst of all," said Basil, "some Old Boy is really pushing for my firing because during one of my shows some woman requested that one of my pieces, *Ophelia, Dead in New Standpipe*, be pulled."

"Ophelia?"

"Because I use my enemy's bullets doesn't mean I belong or I've defected to his camp. So – and don't look at me that way – the woman objected to the supposed homoerotic content of the piece. A reporter from *The Gleaner* asked me to respond. I said as long as I was on top, I didn't care about people's sexual persuasion. Here, read it for yourself, I've saved it for a rainy day when I'm really depressed."

"But it hasn't rained," I said.

"The sprinklers will do," he said and put out his cigarette on the edge of a palette. The heat of the cigarette flared the residue of paint on the palette and Basil killed the flame with the palm of his hand. He then searched through the pile of newspapers and found the article near the bottom. I read aloud the section that was underlined in red ink:

Despite the idyllic, almost pastoral, nature of his landscapes, the paintings retain a tormented air. His most recent paintings, frequently flawed by a gratuitous use of primary colours, are needlessly reworked, which seems out of character with a depiction of paradise. Cunningham, however, still manages to communicate sex and absurdity, perhaps joy, all the stuff of life.

I held the pages in my hands while Basil swilled his drink around in his mouth and swallowed. He took the paper from my hand, threw it on the floor, spilled globs of paint over it and smeared it with his hands.

"Paradise. Shit. Why must everything we do be a depiction of paradise? Anyway, I offended the woman with my painting, and offended the president of the Old Boys Association, Larry Buchanan, who's trying to get me fired because of what I said and because I set a bad example."

"But why would he do that?" I said in disbelief. "Why would he of all people want to get rid of you?"

"Bitch," said Basil, and cleaned his hands on one of the rags. "He wants to protect all of us from ourselves, and I want to be left alone. Guys like him, because of their own guilt, try to make people like me feel as guilty as they do about themselves. They try so hard to control our lives, to try and make us feel guilty for what we are. They try to shame us, and if that doesn't work, they call us mad. Add that to being an artist and you're really asking for trouble!"

"So why don't you leave? You could leave here and live anywhere in the world."

"And miss all this fun? I've fought too hard to be where I am now to give it up and go somewhere else. I know people like the Doc would like me to paint *Waterlilies,* like Monet, but how can I paint like Monet when I know it's some dead ancestor from Benin who's tending the garden so he can paint. I'm interested in the figures outside the frame, the workers who made it possible for the water lilies to bloom. That's why I'm still around. Why I remain a committed Marxist, no matter what."

"I can't believe that you're still a Marxist!"

"You're just saying that because you live in Miami. You can't judge properly because you can't really appreciate your own time. If we produce inferior art, as Doc is always so willing to remind us, then it's because we remain in this feudal slave society governed by American interests, who are determined for us to remain in the Third World while they enter their information age, their New World Order."

"So what are you suggesting?"

"Getting rid of them once and for all and allowing our history to take its true course."

"I know what history does. I know boat people! Anyone who could drive someone to brave those waters is a bigger thug than you or I could imagine."

Basil was surprised. When I was younger, I'd attended the political rallies with him because I thought I was struggling with the poor and downpressed for equal rights, not just in my own country, but in Namibia, Angola, Mozambique,

South Africa, and Rhodesia. I thought I was a young freedom fighter. And war sometimes meant suppressing other rights My high school years were spent fighting for rights, but since then, I'd lost the will or didn't have anything worth fighting for.

Dada had said, "Without freedom, all other values are worthless. You can't fight for freedom by silencing or putting others down." When I got to Miami I saw what he meant. All the discards washed up on the shore: Haitians, Cubans, and Vietnamese, casualties spawned by the so-called "historical process".

"A thug?"

"A bigger one than my friend supposedly is. At least Adrian has the excuse of kids and a family. All *those* monsters had was a craven greed for power. So much for them and history."

Basil stubbed out his cigarette and lit another. Mine had burned out by itself.

There was a knock on the door and then a boy, about the same age as I was when I met Basil, came inside. He was wearing a pair of green flip-flops, a maroon pair of sweat pants and a plaid dress shirt whose tails he had tied around his waist, his navel protruding under the knot. He took one look at me and went up the stairs. He had his own key. Basil turned his dead eye in my direction.

"I'd better be going," I said. I was feeling extremely awkward. "I don't want to be caught in the curfew."

"Nonsense," said Basil. "The curfew doesn't start until nine o'clock and it's only six. And you can always stay here."

"I wish I could," I said.

This was a lie. The boy's looks had spooked me and I think my little speech had rubbed Basil the wrong way. "No I can't stay. Emma has planned a big dinner for me. I can't disappoint her."

"I understand," he said, and he took my glass from me. There was still some rum left and he drank it. There were scars on his wrists.

"Never waste a drop," he said.

He hugged me and I hugged him back and then we walked out into the parking lot. A few more cars had parked near the entrance.

Night was creeping in from Standpipe and the streetlights buzzed to life. Fireflies flitted over the treetops. Women were coming home from their work in New Standpipe, their heels pick-pocking against the sidewalk, the wind toying with the fringes of their skirts. Tired and worn, weighted down by the day's cares – rent, the children, the men who never came home – they dragged their shadows across the hard, uneven pavement. Dark curled around their bodies.

CHAPTER NINE

Down the darkened lane, past the stoops haunted by the rum-heads and mongrels, I headed towards the light of the square where the latest Trench Town prophet was preaching to the crowd, confirming their belief that suffering was a sure sign of our collective sainthood.

"We, we black people are the true children of Gawd," he bellowed. "We, we are the lost tribe of Israel. And all what we going through now is but a passing through the vale of tears. We shall sit at the right hand of Gawd. The first shall be last, and the lame shall enter first..."

The crowd cheered and he continued with his sermon, his theology of woundedness. I left the square and continued to the minibus station.

A rage was rising in my chest. A rage like the mad hurl of those minibuses through the darkness. I shouldn't have come back. In Miami I could have thought about everything in the most idyllic and romantic way, but now I had to confront everyone in the flesh. I was beginning to feel I had lost everything, was losing everything, would lose everything. Again.

Under the zinc roof of the station, a ragged group of stale drunks surrounded by bottles of Red Stripe, half-eaten patties and greasy napkins was sprawled over the benches that circled Carib Theatre. Stragglers from Sabina Park climbed over each other for a space on the minibuses, trying to get home before the curfew began. I spotted an empty seat in a minibus, but a higgler and her basket muscled me out. I decided to walk over to the taxi station further up the road when I heard music coming from a bar on Old Hope Road.

It had begun to drizzle and my T-shirt was getting wet. I thought maybe I could rest there from the confusion of the day. I went inside the bar whose walls were lined with posters of Bob Marley and calendars for Appleton with half-naked women lounging on the beach at Dunn's River Falls with the water surging up between their legs.

I ordered a cold Red Stripe, but the bartender told me he only had hot beers and I figured Red Stripe was a Red Stripe, hot or cold. I asked him to change a twenty-dollar bill so if it came to it, I could take a taxi home. I didn't want to be travelling with a taxi man late at night and flashing American dollars.

I drank the beer slowly, letting the bubbles tickle my tongue. The pain in the side of my mouth was almost gone. I began wondering what Nicole was doing in Miami. Was she in her apartment watching television or in the bathroom combing her hair?

Over in the corner facing the bathroom, a domino game was starting. The bartender walked over to the players and said, "Rain falling and because oonu have car, don't mean oonu can stay here all night. Me have house too. And them police boy nah fool around out on de road tonight. The Prime Minister give them full authority to do whatever them want." Then he turned and in a gentle voice said, "Doris, you want another Dragon?"

Doris looked up at the bartender and nodded, "One more for the road." She had high cheekbones, brown eyes, and her yellow dress brought out the warm tone in her complexion. "Oonu give me rub. Oonu a shuffle the card like oonu have hook worm."

I went over to the jukebox to check the selections. I found an oldie and slipped the dollar into the machine.

Doris shuffled the dominos, and I came closer to her.

"You sure she not coding?"

They all glared at me and she continued shuffling the cards. Finally, she looked up at me. "You been away for a long time, no? The way we play it here, we trust each other. If you can't trust the people you play with, why play at all?"

The man to her right broke in, "The only thing me don't like is when woman rub domino over me head."

"Especially when them winning, eh?" she said.

"Don't rile Malcolm," said her partner.

"Me don't like to get man excited." She rubbed the man's shoulder. "A big strapping man like this, who know what him would do?"

The record slipped on the platter and Ken Boothe, whose voice, the old ballers used to say, could snap a million and one bra straps without anyone touching them, began:

When I fall in love, it will be forever, cause I will never, ever fall in love again...

Doris glanced over at me and said, "You put that on?"

"Yes," I said.

"Good song," she said. I moved closer to her and noticed dreadlocks under her cap. She smelled like fresh cut dahlias.

Doris and the proud conscious movement of her head intrigued me. She had entered their world and was holding her own with them, at their own game. They didn't like it. I wanted more.

I tapped the shoulder of a man with a transistor cradled in his lap and tried to join the circle, "So how many wickets have we lost?"

The man looked at me in my T-shirt, my jeans, my sneakers and said, "Depend on who *we* is."

His partner grinned and Doris shuffled the dominos one more time. Then to ease the tension she said, "You really have to rub these dominoes because domino is like man, a rub here and dub there, and pretty soon you have a full hand."

She backed away and let the men grab their cards.

"That's why you don't have no man," said the man on her right.

"The last one she have was like putty in her hand," said her partner.

"You right, him was like putty in me hand. That's why I don't have no man," she said. "Them cyaan keep up with me, and me will never be beholden to any man. I always haffi hold them hand and guide them through everything. Like my partner this afternoon never want play. Him say him cyaan play domino. I say to him, connect, connect the dots and me take care of the res.'"

"Nuff respect, sister," said her partner.

If I should fall in love again, to me it would be a pleasure, crooned Ken, and Doris rubbed her legs together.

An old sour drunk wandered in from the rain. He shook the rain from a hat he'd made from newspaper and stumbled between the stools until he found his regular spot. He rubbed his rheumy eyes, scratched his buttocks and when he saw Doris, patted his beer belly and shuffled over to the table. He buttoned the top of his shirt, rested his arm on my shoulder and pointed at Doris.

"Pizen," he said, "all of them is pizen. Them no good. Better leave them when you have the chance."

"What you want, Simon?" asked the bartender. "I hope you don't come in here to preach tonight because I tired of you and you preaching."

"But young boys like these must know," said Simon, and he pointed at me, "them must know the evil that is woman. Them must know how woman, with their wiles, will trap man in eternal damnation."

"Old man," said the bartender, "I wouldn't mind getting trapped tonight."

Doris laughed and crossed her legs.

"Is people like you," said Simon, "people like you who going make young boys like these waste their time, their valuable time on Jezebels and harlots."

He inched back to his stool and pushed away one of the wineglasses on the counter. The wineglass crashed to the floor.

Cause I'll never, ever fall in love again...

Nicole where are you? A sour feeling rose in my throat. The old man was numbing his pain the way I once had, pushing drinks down my throat until I couldn't see any more, then playing chicken with the light posts, backing out at the last moment, hoping that a state trooper would pull me up and arrest me on a DUI. But it never happened. So I mixed amphetamines with vodka and went to sleep. My mother found me, put me in the hospital and told me to get help. Then she died.

The bartender rushed over to clean the splinters. Simon hobbled over to the door. He palmed a saltshaker as he left.

"All oonu want is adultery and fornication," he shouted. "First Corinthians six, verse four 'Know ye not that neither fornicators, nor adulterers, nor men who lie with men shall inherit the kingdom of God!'"

"If I get me hand on you," said the bartender, "you gwane inherit the kingdom tonight."

"Fornication," said Simon, "fornication and adultery."

Preachers everywhere. Preachers in every hole of this island.

He spat on the welcome mat and heeled the spit into the grooves.

The bartender scooped the broken glass in a can, pulled off his apron, and came around the counter.

"Take you raas out of me bar and don't come back. If you come back, is dead you going dead!"

Badow! The saltshaker exploded against the front of the counter and the top rolled between my feet.

"Eat! Eat all you want of Lot's wife who desired the lust and fornication of Sodom and Gomorrah! The counterfeit kingdom!"

The bartender ran outside, but Simon had already disappeared into the rain. My legs were trembling against the stool. I gulped down the rest of the beer.

"You all right, youth man?" asked the bartender. "Him lick you?"

"I'm okay," I said and left a dollar under the coaster.

"You is an American, nuh," said the bartender.

"Why do you say that?" I asked.

"You left a tip," he explained. He went around the counter and put on his apron. "You better get back to you hotel quick. Curfew. It gwane dread tonight."

It was no use explaining anything. I looked around the bar. It was empty. Ken Boothe sang the last note and his voice faded into the static of the bartender's broom against the terrazzo tile.

"Papine, Papine, here," cried the conductor of the jitney that pulled up outside the bar. The jitney had a space for one beside the conductor and I jumped in. It wasn't going exactly my way, but it was getting late and I could walk across the main road through Mona Heights and call Chris from the pay phone in the community centre.

The bus lurched towards the Old Hope Road, through the roads lined with nightclubs and cold supper shops that were closed for the night. The rain was coming down in buckets and the jitney's wipers were frantically sweeping the water back and forth. The boulevard's sodium brightness burned into my eyes. There was nowhere to hide. It was dread.

CHAPTER TEN

So old man river don't you cry for me, I've got a running stream of love you see, sang Papa Legba as his voice boomed through the kiosk at the Mona Centre where I waited for a taxi to take me home. The phones at home were busy when I'd called about an hour before and it was safer to take a taxi from Mona than Cross Roads. When I saw Papa Legba I walked over to the fence, lifted the line of barbed wire and he came into the park.

Water ran down the bald clay escarpment, loosening gravel and sandstone around the central pole of the kiosk. The night drowsed between the hills.

"Hail, Benjamin," he said. "I man glad to see the I don't lose faith. The race is not for the weak, but for the I that I-dureth for I-ver."

We went back over to the wooden bench under the kiosk. From there I could see the traffic from the boulevard and any cars that were entering or leaving the park. A single bulb that hung from the rafter illuminated the walkway. Six cars entered the park through the top gate, and four came into it from the west gate and parked on the opposite side of the building. Something was happening in the centre.

"So how are you, Papa Legba?"

"I man irie, irie irie," he said and by the redness of his eyes I knew he was telling the truth. "So what the I a deal with?"

He laid his staff on the bench and sat on the table around the supporting pole, pulling his tunic between his legs.

"I'm doing all right," I said, "but you've been deceiving me."

"Deceive the I? I an I is no Satan? How I deceive the I?"

"Enough double-talk, Papa Legba."

"I man speak the truth and so must the I. That is the first step to man-tain the I I-tegrity."

"Why didn't you tell me that Adrian was in trouble, that he had killed Dada?"

"I man don't know who the I talking about," he said.

"Okay. Why didn't you tell me that Reuben killed Dada?"

"Who say Reuben kill your father?"

"The police, the news..."

"And you believe everything the news and police tell you?"

"No, but..."

"So why you believe them now? Jah-son, the I know the truth. These things is the works of Satan. Don't believe them. They tell you what they want you to hear, what they want you to know. But the I know the truth. Don't make men and people tell you different. For what has been hidden from the wise and the prudent is now revealed to the babe and the suckling. Many shall be called, but few shall be chosen."

"And you are one of the chosen? Papa Legba, I don't have to tell you, but a lot of people think you're quite mad."

He dug inside his tunic, pulled out a bud the size of his hand and sniffed it. It was as red as the star on his shirt. He searched his pockets for his knife and cut off a piece.

"Tell I who mad Jah-son. Behold, the rain falling, the river flowing and still Jah children cyaan get a cool drink of water. Now that is real madness."

"Papa Legba," I said, "you know the reason for the water shortages is that the rain isn't falling in the catchment areas and the river alone can't supply the city's demand. It's always been that way."

"That is the lie that Babylon television and newspaper been feeding your mind since you was youth. Who create

142

shortage to raise the price? Who tell you there is nothing when there is always something for Jah children? The drought is in men's minds. Whatever a man I-sire, so shall it be. The real drought is because sin has entered the garden of Jah. This is the dream of Babylon that I and I let go a long time now."

"You call this the garden of Jah? Children running around with bloated bellies and flies buzzing around their heads. People stabbing and shooting each other."

"And who making brethren kill brethren, sistren killing sistren? Babylon, the mother of harlots. Queen Elizabitch, and all the nations of the earth that tell the children that Selassie I is not their father. That tell the children they have no father but the white God in heaven. These are the same men who rage war against the Lamb, and tell the children that they are less than nothing, who beat down the children every day with their lies. What cause this drought but fear? Babylon telling the children that in Jah earth there is never enough for everyone, so some must eat and some must go hungry."

He cleaned the stalk and separated the seeds from the twigs. He chopped the leaves then scooped them into a piece of Bambu rolling paper. Balancing the herb in the middle of the paper, he rolled then licked and sealed the end of the spliff.

"Sight Benjamin. Earth is like this herb. Every living thing have it own seed and multiply after it own kind. The youth can't know Oneself. This island killing the youth every day by fooling them so they can't trust their own feelings. Everyone know the herb is good. Everyone know that sex is good. But they want to kill the promised seed with the edge of the sword, in their family planning, in their birth control to kill black people."

"Don't tell me you're still against birth control," I said. "Can't you see the pain in this country cause by overpopulation and mindless breeding?"

"Mind-less breeding is right," he interrupted. "Breeding

and breathing without love, without life. They downbeating this island like this island is not a part of them, like them is not a part of this island. They will have to know that not a thing don't move without Jah love. The I know Jah love, Benjamin?"

The lights went on around the centre and the shrill sound of feedback from a microphone tore through the windows.

"So if they'll have to pay, why can't we prevent the misery? Why weren't you around when my father was being killed."

"Ah, Benjamin, the questioner," he said. "The questions. The questions. From you was youth it was always the same way. Questions, questions! Always using you wizzy. But Benjamin, the I haffi see Jah light, for if the I don't discern Jah truth from darkness, then I word will have fallen on barren soil. The I haffi see that is these men and people make this hell hole, as you call it, the way it is and them could change everything tomorrow if them did want. But them don't want to. Instead of doing what Jah put them on this earth to do, they waiting for someone to tell them what to do. Them prefer filthy lucre to the pain of them brethren. The I cyaan change that, so the I haffi protect oneself from these men and people."

He lit a match and allowed the flame to burn the sulfur residue off the match. He closed his eyes in a prayer, then put the spliff in his mouth and cupped his palm over the flame. He inhaled and the few seeds that were left in the spliff exploded and fell in a puddle beside the kiosk.

Three more cars, followed by a black sedan, and then two more cars entered through the western gate.

"Aren't you afraid of being arrested? It's still against the law isn't it?"

"What law? Men law. Babylon law, but never against the law of Jah. What is true now, will remain true for I-ver."

"You could get into a lot of trouble for believing that. If the police catch you, they'll lock you up and my father isn't around to save you any more."

He smiled when I said "my father". He picked up his staff and made seven holes in the mud. He filled his hand with the seeds he had gathered from cleaning the herb and dropped them in the holes. The seeds floated for a second, then sank into the mud.

"The greatest jail is a man's mind. Him see wall where there are none, him see scarcity where there is abundance. I mind free. Jah son, the I must free up the I mind."

He covered the seeds with his staff and cleaned the mud off the bottom.

"Grow herb seed, grow, for unless a seed fall into the earth, how shall it bear fruit?"

The smoke from his spliff billowed over my head and seemed to suspend itself almost solidly under the naked bulb. He bowed his head, took off his tam and shook his dreadlocks. They dangled lazily over his shoulders.

"That's all well and good for you to say, but I'm really afraid of what they'll do to you if they catch you. You're not young any more, you know."

"Young, old, living, dead. The I use words that I and I don't overstand. For if the I have the faith of a herb seed, then Jah will be done. Humble yourself. For I and I don't need no light but Jah Son, Jah moon and Jah stars. Don't need no electric but Jah love in I soul. Babylon try to dull I senses, but all I want is sinsemilla. I and I don't need the pleasure of the world, the pleasures of Babylon."

"Don't knock the pleasures of the world till you've tried them," I said. "They can open your eyes to more things than you've dreamed about."

"I and I open until I can see that everything is vanity and a chasing after the wind."

Then he turned and looked me straight in the eyes, "Stop polluting your temple with wine and strong drink. Is holy work the I put in him father vineyard to do. Receive the blessings of I father through the power of the herb for the I is truly blessed."

Before I could say anything, he patted me on the arm and shoved a spliff into my left pocket.

"I don't smoke this any more," I said. But for the first time in about ten years I was tempted. Papa Legba grew and smoked his own herb and never sold even a bud to anyone. His herb was clean. I decided to keep the spliff.

"Stand firm," he said. "Babylon!" He tramped through the mud and under the fence.

Headlights flashed through the kiosk and a police jeep came inside the park. Before I had time to throw away the spliff, a police officer jumped out off the jeep and a soldier with an M-16 stayed behind. He gripped the handle of his revolver as he came into the kiosk and shone a flashlight in my face.

"What you name?"

"Jason Stewart," I said out of habit. I couldn't see his face.

"You see a Rasta who call himself Papa Legba around here."

"No, I'm here alone."

I pushed the spliff deeper into my pocket.

"You sure," he said. "Because we had a report that him was here. What you doing here?"

"I'm waiting for a taxi."

The policeman snickered, "No taxi gwane come get you. You better find youself a nice Jamaican girl for the night."

"I think I'll call home," I said, and got up off the bench. I walked nervously past him and the soldiers to the front of the community centre. There were at least thirty cars parked at the side of the building.

The police officer followed me to the front door. I stuck my head in the door. Something was happening inside. A few reporters, some of my old teachers from Jamaica College, and shaggy professors from the university, sandalled socialists who had lived out their own stereotypes, were sitting around the platform and clapping gleefully. The platform was draped with red and black streamers and a banner: One God, One Leader, One Aim, One Destiny. Carmichael, the old charmer, was lecturing them and up to his old tricks. They were hooked on his every word, every subtle casual gesture, like children watching a magician and trying to live inside his illusions.

Carmichael continued his speech in a slower cadence.

"And now let me say something that goes to the heart of our situation, my brothers and sisters. What we are facing is a crisis that will have a profound impact on our society."

He cradled them in his arms and they loved it as he worked them into a fever.

"We are facing corruption that is like a worm eating away the vitality of our nation. If we allow it to continue, we will be like dry cane husk, used and abused and thrown into the fire."

I tried to slip in behind the audience when Larry spotted me. He looked as if someone had died. He was sloppier than usual and his hair was completely frazzled.

"But the worst part, my brothers and sisters, is that instead of resisting this corruption, this new white death," Carmichael continued, "this next slavery that comes as powder, as a rock, as a stone, we are embracing it, galloping headlong to our destruction. We are tolerating violence to ourselves, to our soul, and this, I suggest, is a lunatic mode of existence. But we cannot combat this alone. *We* have to act together. *We* have to give up this image of ourselves as cowboys, making up the rules as we go along. *We* have to change from being a nation of loners to becoming a nation. *We* have to solve the disconnection between our personal actions and collective consequences."

I couldn't listen any more. I'd heard speeches like this before and they were all the same: a combination of working-class rhetoric, Rasta theology and Protestant revulsion against sin spun into a neat tale of fall and redemption. Carmichael had said these lines a thousand times and he was now merely an actor repeating lines that neither he nor his audience believed, but it felt good so they came for another show.

"What are you doing here?" asked Larry. He seemed surprised to see me.

"Come to use the phone."

"I mean, what are you doing here? Everybody's been looking for you since you disappeared in Standpipe. Your brother, Emma, they've all been calling Carmichael."

"I went to see Adrian," I said.

"Oh," he said, "I'll soon be back. Wait for me here."

Larry went around the side of the community centre and came back with a bottle of Appleton and two glasses. We walked back to the kiosk and sat on the bench. Larry poured himself a drink.

"You want one?" and he poured some into the other glass.

"No," I said. "I've had my quota for the day."

"Suit yourself," he said and poured the rum into his glass. "So did you see Adrian?"

"Didn't you hear he was arrested for killing my father?"

"I heard, but I wasn't sure you had."

"Is it true?"

"Yes. From what I've heard from my sources in the police, Adrian did it."

"But why?"

Larry and Reuben had never been friends. They had circled each other cautiously like two dangerous animals that were deadly enemies, but never attacked, out of respect for each other's ferocity.

"He has three children, you know. You can't feed children by being an ex-soccer star. I tried to help him to get a job, but he never wanted help. Didn't want any help from a batty man. He never liked me. He hated Damien and I because we were gay. Do you remember when he put the fibreglass in my underwear?"

"The fibreglass was funny," I said. "But he did it because you guys noosed his balls to his bed post. You could have hurt him. And he didn't hate you because you were gay. He hated you because you always thought you were better than everyone else."

"What made him think that?"

"You have it in your veins, Larry. You don't know when

148

you're being condescending. It's in your veins. I never thought you had a problem with being gay. I always said you had a problem with being white."

"And you with being brown," he shot back.

"So we're two bastards," I said.

"And you're the bigger one," he said.

"I'm not too sure about that these days," I said. "I went to see Basil."

Wonder of wonders. Larry was speechless. He brushed back his hair from out of his face, and I noticed a bald spot. He was going to be as bald as his father was before he reached his mid-thirties.

"So what does Basil have to say for himself these days?"

"He tells me you're trying to get him fired from Jamaica College. I told him I couldn't believe you would do something like that."

"You better believe it," he said firmly. "I wish we'd fired him a long time ago."

"How can you say that! How can you be firing him? I mean it's no big secret about you and Damien."

"Don't bring Damien into this!" he snapped. "The first time you said his name I let it go, but I'm not going to let you get away with it a second time."

"Because I didn't come to his funeral?"

"The funeral is not one tenth of it," he said, "not one tenth of it."

He held the glass tightly, sipped his rum, then climbed up on the table and rested his head against the pole.

"Let's drop it," he said. "Have a rum with me."

"I won't drop it," I said. "But okay, I'll have a rum with you."

"That's more like it," he said and uncapped the bottle. He poured me about two fingers.

"So are you going to tell me why you're mad with me?"

"I'm not mad at you," he said. "I have a lot on my mind."

"Like what?"

"You'll soon hear," he said. "You'll soon hear."

"I may be leaving tomorrow," I said.

"Then I guess you won't hear," he said unapologetically.

"What's up, Larry? You think that I've sold out in America, don't you? That I've somehow changed. I haven't changed. I'm the same old Jason."

"But which Jason are you? Are you Jason, my friend, Jason the young protégé of Basil Cunningham? Jason, the young Rastafarian? Or Jason whatever you've become in America? What happened to you, Jason? The Jason I know would never have left me to bury our friend alone." He stressed the word "our".

"So that's it," I said, holding back my anger. As if he was the only one who grieved when Damien died, as if his love for Damien made Damien exclusive property. I sipped my drink. It didn't hurt any more.

"You're mad at me because I didn't come back for Damien's funeral, but I had a lot going on in my life too. Did you think about that? But that doesn't excuse what you're doing to Basil!"

"One thing has nothing to do with the other," he said calmly. "And if you really want to know, I'm trying to get rid of Basil because of what he's doing to the college. He's a paedophile, Jason. He seduces those pathetic little boys from Standpipe who need some sort of father figure in their lives. I'm having a hard enough time getting money from the Old Boys for upkeep. You've seen the place."

"How did you know I was there?"

"Who, in the first place, do you think bent Carmichael's ear so you could get there. I told him to give you the clearance. I wanted you to see how dilapidated the place has become. If you decide to come back and live we need you on our side."

"It really is bad," I said, deflecting his plea.

"And it's going to get worse," said Larry. "Too many Old Boys have given up their responsibility to Jamaica College. Do you realize how many people didn't get a chance at an education while we went there? Do you know how much of this country's resources went into educating us, how many people went to bed hungry at night so we could sit in the Great Room and argue whether Camus provided a more elegant thesis on the existential crisis of the twentieth century or whether Descartes' ontological position was defensible? In this country, it's I eat therefore I live."

"It's not that simple," I said, "especially when your talent and intelligence, as is Basil's case, leads you to question the basic assumptions that our country works on. The answers to questions like what makes us so poor? And don't give me the bullshit about colonialism, slavery, and neo-colonialism. We've had as much to do with our poverty as the colonialists."

"But Basil, instead of being an asset, has become a liability. People are already homophobic, and I can't get a cent because he's there. He's only thinking about himself. He has to go."

"I didn't know you were so powerful."

Larry hung his head between his legs and a low gurgling sound came from his throat. He climbed down off the table, finished his drink and put the glass on the table.

"As they say in Standpipe, me big a yard."

I took another sip. Now there was only a feeling like a dull pressure, an absence.

Applause broke out in the centre and then there was a silence that lasted about fifteen seconds, then more frantic applause, and then a wail.

"I guess Carmichael has told them," said Larry.

"Told them what?"

"He's retiring," said Larry.

"But why? He looks fit enough to go on for another ten years."

"Hodgkin's disease," said Larry. "We got the diagnosis last week. He waited until after your father's funeral to make the announcement to our party stalwarts."

"Speaking of diagnoses," I hesitated.

"Negative," he paused, "so far. But we'll see."

I finished my drink and gave him my glass. What more

could I say, he was my friend. We marched around to the front of the community centre, arm in arm, like the old days when we launched campaigns against the radio stations for hiring DJs who sounded as if they were from Detroit rather than Denham Town.

Larry went back to his car to put away the bottle of rum and the glasses.

Outside the centre, four men with the party flag draped over their shoulders were sitting on the steps, comforting each other. Inside, a woman who was stacking the chairs, stopped, let the chair fall to the floor and began sobbing uncontrollably. A listlessness had overtaken the hall. No one, except the reporters who had all lined up by the phone, wanted to do anything.

Carmichael saw me and I walked over to him.

"Jason, Emma's been calling me all day about you." And when he saw my face he said, "I suppose you heard."

"Does Emma know?"

"I told her yesterday," said Carmichael. "That's why I visited her."

He pulled me beside him. His bodyguards were holding supporters at arm's length, but they couldn't stop some from patting him on his shoulder and touching the hem of his jacket. Larry joined us.

"We have to get you home, young man," Carmichael said. "I saw Emma at Sabina today and she's really worried about you."

"I know, I promised her I'd be home for dinner," I said.

"I promised her I'd find you," he said, "but I'm sorry I can't take you home myself. I have to work out some things with Larry before tomorrow morning and before those vultures get hold of my story."

"I understand," I said.

Turning to Larry he said, "You drove your car, right?"

"Yes."

"Okay," he said and turned to me. "Victor, my driver will take you home." He called to his driver. "Victor, I want you to take Jason home. You know where his house is. This is Albert Lumley's son. Jagga will drive the car and Larry is going with me back to the house. Take good care of him," he said.

"I'll get the car," said Larry

While we waited for Larry to get his car, a few more supporters came out to the centre. One woman, weak from wailing, could barely walk, and was supported by two men. They tried to come near Carmichael, but his bodyguards stopped them.

"I feel like I've betrayed them," he said. "They believed in me so much."

"You need to take care of yourself," I said. "After you're better you can come back."

"No," he said firmly. "This is it for me. I'm leaving this for the younger ones who have the stomach for it."

He looked over the top of Jack's Hill, dotted with stars, and said, "You know, it started so innocently. We said we wanted to be free, we needed to protect ourselves. Now look at us, we have to be protecting ourselves from ourselves. That it should come to this, brothers killing brothers. No, I can't come back to this, and especially now with this illness, I feel I've given my life to this country for all the wrong reasons."

"How can you say that?"

"What do I have to show after all these years?" he said wistfully.

"You helped to free a nation. Isn't that enough?"

"I know that," he said. "But I think about your father, his family, Emma, two sons. He was the luckier one."

Then a bitter laugh slipped out of him. "His death saved my life. You know if he hadn't died, I'd still be going a few more rounds with him. I'd probably have put off the treatment to spar a bit longer with him. He was a good fighter."

"Is that your only regret?"

"No, my only regret is that I couldn't do more. That

we're so poor and every time we try to grow out of poverty something new comes along. Every time we get a dollar and we think we can build a new school, we have to spend it to service our debts, to give the poor HIV treatments, to fight narco-traffickers. And before you look around, we're further in debt. And it's no use asking our friends to the north. They say it's not their problem, that it's a local problem. But we don't make guns in this island. HIV didn't start in this island; cocaine didn't start in this island. All of that came from the north and it's not their problem?"

I'd heard that speech too many times. I tried to change the subject.

"So what are you going to do now?"

"Enjoy my friends, go to cricket matches, and write my memoirs," he said.

"Then you have another lifetime's work ahead of you," I said.

"Thank you, Jason," he said. "Your father didn't deserve a son like you."

Larry drove up in a beaten up Lada and left the engine running. Victor looked at the car in disgust. Carmichael shook my hand and Larry got in Carmichael's car with Jagga and Butto.

"I'll call Emma from my car phone and tell her you're on the way," said Carmichael. "Victor will take good care of you."

The lights in the centre went off one by one, the speakers taken away. The flags and streamers were lowered and the banners stuffed into the back of a pickup truck. When we left the centre, the park was quiet, a hollow shell littered with paper cups and posters.

We got in the car and Victor turned down Gerbera Drive towards Matilda's Corner.

Victor, a small bald-headed man with a huge potbelly and short stumpy arms, mumbled something that at first I didn't hear, for I was too busy trying to put together the events of the day. Everything was happening faster than I could understand. By the time we'd reached the foot of Beverly Hills, I was lost in thought, hypnotized by the lights of August Town as they slithered around Wareika, a galaxy drawn by the thread of stars hovering over the blackness of Hope River.

"What were you saying? I'm sorry I didn't hear you."

"What you worry about so much, boss," he said. "Everything going be all right. Once you with me, you safe! You born a foreign, right?"

"No, I was born here, but I left a long time ago. I live in Miami now."

"So you here to stay?"

"No, I'm leaving tomorrow."

"You must stay, boss. Me did have a chance to go a Florida one time and work in the sugar field, but me couldn't take it. If me go to America, me is just a black man, not that me shame of being a black man. But in Jamaica me is just Victor, nothing more, nothing less. So me stay and with the piece of land me have in the hills, me have a bar and a small shop."

"So how come you ended up being Uncle David's driver?"

"Me cyaan take the stay home business. The Bible say a man must do what him have to do, and me love the road. What sweeter in life, besides a Jamaican woman, than driving through the countryside? The up and down, the haul and pull up, the wash way and draw you brakes. Is me should pay him for a job so sweet."

Victor popped the clutch and slipped into a lower gear. As we came around the corner, floodlights momentarily blinded him and he let go of the steering wheel. The car swerved out of control and skidded across the road towards a barricade manned by two soldiers. Victor steered in the direction of the skid, corrected, and pulled up the hand brake and the car spun in the opposite direction.

Before we knew what was happening, soldiers with machine guns scrambled down the side of the hill and pointed their guns in the window. A police officer slammed his hand against the roof of the car.

"Out of the car, now. The two of you, move it!" he barked

"Boss, me is..." but before Victor could finish the sentence, the policeman pulled out his gun and pointed it in his face, "I ask you anything?"

We got out of the car and I followed Victor's lead. I held my arms over my head and leaned against the car.

The soldiers searched Victor, but found nothing except a flyer announcing Carmichael's speech at the centre.

"So oonu is thief or batty man? For is only thief or batty man out at this time of night?"

A policeman searched my waist, legs and the small of my back. He ran his gun across my chest and searched my right pocket. He found my wallet. He pulled out the news article, and held it up to the light and put it back in my pocket. He searched my left pocket and pulled out the spliff. I'd forgotten about that. He handed it to a sergeant who came over to interrogate me.

"What is this? What is this, pretty boy? Ganja? Is smoking you smoking ganja. You going to jail, you going to jail tonight, pretty boy," said the sergeant. His nostrils flared and his neck, covered with razor bumps and red pustules, seemed as if they were going to ooze with blood at any moment.

I was going to drop my father's name, but by the way they treated Victor I didn't know whose side they were on. One false move and the two of us could have been dead. It was best to keep silent.

"It's not mine. Papa Legba gave it to me," I said without thinking.

"Papa Legba! You know Papa Legba, pretty boy? We searching for him all night. I want to drill him backside full of lead. Tell me where him is and we set you free right here."

"I don't know where he is and if I did..."

I wasn't going to betray another friend.

"Is facesty, you want facesty with me boy?" A policeman clubbed me on the side of my head, and I fell to the ground. Victor tried to move towards me, but the soldiers restrained him.

"Make me jus shat the boy, sah. Make me jus shat him. Teach him some respect!"

The police ransacked Larry's car, under the seats, behind the back seats, the ashtray and behind the dashboard. They opened the trunk and the hood, but couldn't find anything except bottles of rum and vodka.

The sergeant came over to Victor and said, "We going let you go. You better check the wiring in this car. And put some water in the radiator. The fancy driving you do overheat the engine. We should arrest you for improper vehicular maintenance, but these Lada don't worth a fart, and jail full tonight."

"Is not my car, boss."

"Don't argue with me," said the sergeant.

Victor closed the hood and the trunk, then got in the car and started the engine. The soldiers removed the barricade and the police officer directed him through gauntlet of soldiers.

"So where you taking the boy?" Victor asked.

"None of your fucking business," said the sergeant.

"Me responsible for the boy," said Victor.

"Matilda's Corner," said the sergeant. "And if you ask any more question I might just let loose my friend with the gun."

"And what him can do?"

"You better go on you way fast, you hear me. If we shat you out here who you think going miss you? Who you think going find you? Only john crow. Shut you mouth an go on bout you business."

He motioned to the soldier. I was still groggy and the soldier lifted me to my feet and handcuffed me. He dragged me over to a squad car.

Victor drove past the barricades and the police car where I was being held. The lights pulsed like a heartbeat. My shoulders ached and the handcuffs pressed coldly against my wrists. They lowered my head and pushed me into the back seat of the squad car. The sergeant jumped in the front seat and we headed down Liguanea Avenue to the lockup.

When we arrived at the station, the sergeant took me through the office, and handed me over to another officer who escorted me out to the lockup. Removing my handcuffs, the sergeant shoved me inside the cell while the other policeman stood by the door and covered his face with a handkerchief.

"You lucky the lockup full tonight. This is the luxury suite for our special guest," said the sergeant. "Don't worry about that boy in there, him won't hurt you. Him harmless for the rest of the night. We take care of that."

"Can I make a phone call?" I said in the best American accent that I had perfected over the years and had used to sell so many useless baubles to my gullible customers.

"Phone call?" he said. "Phone call? You been watching too much television in America."

"It's my right," I said. "I have to call home to at least let them know where I am."

"Tomorrow you can do that."

"It's my right! I demand to make a phone call. It's my right. I'm an American citizen."

"Demand? What you talking about demand. Demand what? You think you have any rights? You is a criminal. You lose all your rights inside here. If you want rights, obey the law." He closed the door.

"What are you charging me with?" I called after him.

Through the peephole in the door, I could see them walking up the path to the station, slapping each other on the back. I shouted again and one policeman came back and called out so the sergeant could hear, " You is an American, nuh? American citizen. Well, drop you pants and make you partner in there Miranda you raas. And you can tell that to you Amnesty International. Tell them. Tell them that them can kiss mi raas."

The sergeant laughed, then they both howled.

Their laughter grew fainter and when they finally reached the station and closed the door behind them, everything was quiet. Only the dull whir of the electric generator behind the lockup broke the silence.

CHAPTER ELEVEN

I'd thought Dade County Jail was bad. This lock-up was seven feet by nine with two small air vents – one in the door and one in the back of the wall for ventilation. A huge banyan blocked most of the light that could have come in through the door. The floors were built on a slope so water, urine and other liquid waste drained to the lower end, where cockroaches crawled through the muck.

With all my running, I'd ended up in the very place I was running from. I should have just stood still. If I hadn't been so scared, I would have laughed.

I tried to call to the policemen again, but they were too far way, "Please, please let me out of here," I pleaded.

A low retching sound came from the back of the cell, "Save your breath, Benjamin."

I stepped back. It was Reuben.

"Don't worry, Benjamin. You forget who is your brethren? Plus, I cyaan stand up too straight," he said. "I think they really broke me foot this time."

The thought of Reuben hurt made me lose all my fear. I searched through the darkness and found him huddled in a corner. I tried to give him my hand to lift him up, but he brushed it away.

"Reuben, what have they done to you?" I asked.

He tried to speak, but ended up crying. He cleared his throat, spat on the floor, then took a deep breath.

"Nothing them won't do to you if you tell them who you is. Jason, you need to get out of this place fast. I don't think them realize the mistake them make."

"You need to come with me. I'm not leaving without you."

"Me all right," he said. "Me and Papa Legba work out a plan. But it cyaan work, with your blood on me hand." Then he paused, "And with your father blood on me hand."

"You didn't know he was my father," I said. "Don't blame yourself for something you didn't know."

"Like Papa Legba say, me pull the trigger, but me never load the gun."

"What do you mean?" I asked.

Reuben shifted in the corner. I moved to my left. It sounded as if he was moving a bucket closer to him. I bent down beside him and cradled him in my arms. He felt like a long bone wrapped in tattered cloth.

"I never come in the deal to kill you father till late. The last minute. A youth get arrested for herb and Desmond did need a driver. Me wasn't to be a part of it. But me did need the money, so me get in on it."

He tried to straighten out his leg, but winced.

"When the bullet start fly, all me could do was shoot back. Me was only supposed to be the driver. Desmond never expect him to have a gun, but when you father pull out him own gun and shat him, then all me could do was fire back and him dead."

"But how did you get mixed up with someone like that in the first place?"

"Like what, Jason? A whole heap of them is people like you and me. Desmond used to go to Jamaica College, but him couldn't get no work when him tell anybody him come from Standpipe. When me come back from England, after them use me up, I come back here. Me and Desmond used to sell herb to the tourists, then crack, then anything them want."

"So why didn't you take help from Larry when he offered?"

"Who tell you that?"

"Larry."

"That batty boy?"

"Why are you so hard on him? He told me he tried to help you, but you refused."

"Refused? Is him and him batty boy friend get me mixed up in the crack business. We start out with weed after the football match, then we'd pick up some girls at Dizzy's and is there it start. Them boys' hand was too clean to touch the crack themselves, so them get them pyaka to get it for them. Me was them boy. Whenever them batty boyfriend come down from the States, is me go out inna the streets and get it for them. One of them did try poke me. I should have shat him right there. Maybe if a did shoot him, maybe Damien would still be alive. I did like Damien. Him was a good guy."

"And you?"

The breeze shifted the branches of the banyan and the light from the station fell directly on Reuben's face. He had a gash across his forehead to his temple, and his crown was a matted tangle of bloodied hair.

"Me," he said, "me is a dead man. Everybody want me dead. That's why me getting so much licks. Them want to find out what me know. But make me tell you something, you in a whole heap of trouble and you don't know it. As Papa Legba say, you in the den of lion and you don't know. Make me tell you in the simplest way. Chris, your brother, is the one who set up your father."

My mouth went dry.

"But why..." I stuttered.

"Chris was gwane end up here in jail," said Reuben. "Your father never jester when it come to drugs. Him was gwane put him own son in jail for drugs, trafficking in cocaine."

I swallowed hard. It made sense. Chris and I grew up fearing the law that my father wielded like some Old Testament God. Faced with my father prosecuting him without any partiality and the threat of real jail time, Chris, I knew, was capable of anything.

"But why was he trafficking in drugs? He has all the money he could ever want, and if he wanted more, he could always get it from my father."

"Me don't know, Jason. Him love the high life and is like everything to him is a joke. But sometimes a joke can turn serious all of sudden, and when it get serious and him couldn't take the heat, is like him panic, for him realize you father never jester about drugs."

"How do you know this?"

"I tell you is him hire Desmond. Desmond was moving the cocaine through the hotel for Chris."

"But Desmond was PNP? How did they end up together?"

"What better way to hide everything? Desmond and me was from Standpipe, but we did go Jamaica College. And there was money. And there was the cocaine. Coke don't have no pity. It don't have no mother, nor father. It only have itself."

"He smokes crack?"

"No," said Reuben. "Him too smart for that." His voice took on a note of desperation, "But Lawd, Jason, I so sorry. I really never know him was your father. I would never do anything to hurt you. You was me only friend at Jamaica College. You was the only one who never walk around with your nose in the air like you was better than everybody else."

"What are you sorry about? I didn't know the man. I spent all my time in boarding school or with my mother during the holidays. Everyone here seems to be interested in some kind of payback, but I don't care about that. I'm interested in you. But why didn't you say anything about me when they were expelling you?"

"You are me idren, Benjamin. Plus, what me was going do when me graduate from Jamaica College? Work inna office and have some powder batty middle class boy tell me to kiss him ass every day. When me was playing ball, me was the happiest man alive."

"When we were playing ball, you mean. Reuben, as far as

I'm concerned, you killed a stranger. I didn't have any choice over him coming into my life, but I had a choice with you. You can't blame yourself for something you didn't know."

"Yeah, but like Papa Legba say, 'Know or don't know there are things man mustn't do.' And him right."

"Yeah, but Papa Legba's not had the experience we've had."

"How you know that," he said. "You know him was singer. Him used to work as a entertainer, singing calypso and doing magic tricks on a cruise ship that used to go around the islands. They used to call him Calypso Quashie."

Keys clanged outside the door. I could see the officer who had arrested me. He shook the cell door furiously as the keys rattled inside the lock.

"Benjamin," Reuben whispered, "tell my baby mother and my children I'm all right."

"I will," I said.

The cell door swung open and the sergeant charged inside the cell and grabbed me by the arm.

"Get up," he said. "Get up now!"

Before he closed the door, I saw Reuben crouched in the corner, blood splattered and beaten into the ground as if he was nothing, and it broke my heart.

The sergeant saw my reaction and spat on the ground. "Don't waste you tears pan these nasty Rastas," he said. "They get what coming to them."

I was too choked up to answer him.

"Anyway, why you never tell we you was with Mr. Carmichael? You never have to come here if you did tell we the truth instead of all this fuckry about American citizen."

We walked through the back of the station, and the other policeman dusted off my T-shirt and brushed whatever grime he could off my pants. I let him do it because he seemed to be concerned that I was in good shape. We went out to the reception area where Victor met me and escorted me to the car.

"Don't worry about a thing, boss. I tell Mr. Carmichael

that it was the police who plant the weed on you. That them did want money from you."

"You shouldn't have said that; it wasn't the truth," I said.

"Me was only trying to protect you, boss."

"Don't call me boss, Call me Jason or nothing at all." I shouldn't have snapped at him, but he was the only one there.

"Boss, I mean, Mr. Jason, we need to get you up to the house. Somebody, your girl friend, waiting for you up at the house."

At first I didn't believe him, but after what had happened that day anything seemed possible. I said, "If Nicole's there, let's go."

We jumped in the car and Victor raced up a road behind Beverly Hills. I'd never taken this route before. It was still under construction, but it was in better shape than the main roads.

"When did they build this?" I asked Victor.

"A few years ago, boss."

There was no use arguing with him, he would never stop calling me boss.

"It start, then stop, then start again and stop again until a judge rule on the case."

We were near the crest of Wareika and I could see Dada's house and all of Standpipe. Kingston glimmered in the distance: an irregular pattern of lights, like the odd pulse made by the powdery wings of the moths floating blindly through the trees.

A light flickered above the car's speedometer and the engine sputtered and shut down. Victor coasted as far as the momentum could take the car and parked over on the side of the road.

"Boss, is like somebody put obeah on you. You need a sea bath to take all of this bad luck off you."

Victor got out of the car and opened the hood. Steam spewed from the cap of the radiator.

"I tell you," he said, "them want to run the country and

them cyaan run them own car. We haffi go down the hill again. We will call for Mr. David car."

"But I can see my house from here," I said. "I'm going."

"Me not going cross them bad land at night," he said. "Too much Rasta in these hills to cross on foot."

"I used to take this as a short cut when I used to go bird shooting."

"Old time people say short cut still draw blood. Me not going there by night."

"I thought you were here to protect me."

"Me can only protect you body."

"I'm going. Are you coming?"

He tried to hold my arm, but when I saw he wasn't coming, I ran down the hill towards my house. If Nicole was there, I wanted to see her. I had never wanted to see her more desperately in my life.

Branches tore at my shirt as I fought my way through the copse. Whistling toads croaked from the underbrush and screech owls hooted from the treetops.

"Benjamin, Benjamin, me son."

"Papa Legba? Is that you?"

"Benjamin, who shall ravin like wolf by day and share the fruit of his labour by night with his brethren. Blessed be the name of Benjamin, Selah."

"Papa Legba, cut it out!" I shouted.

A dog snarled. Then others. A pack was coming in my direction. I tried to run to the nearest tree with low hanging branches.

"Benjamin, the beloved."

The dogs were getting closer and their growls were more intense. I could see the floodlights near the garage. I was so near. If I made it past the silkcotton tree, I would be home.

The dogs sounded as if they were at my ankles and as I glanced over my shoulder to see how near they were, a dog ran through my legs. It felt as if he'd been trained to do this. I fell face first into the mud. I tried to lift myself up, but the wet leaves slipped over my palms and I fell again into the mud.

There was a thud near my head. A plastic bag filled with papers and something heavy plopped down into the soft leaves. I tried to get up again, but Papa Legba put his staff against my spine.

"Don't get up," he said, and he drew a circle around my body. I still tried to get up, but one of his dogs growled over my head. I stayed down.

"This house is where time begin. Is here your navel string bury, under this silkcotton tree where I and I forefather did hang at the hand of the I forefather."

"What does this have to do with me?" I asked.

"This is the I heritage, Benjamin. Time moving in circles. The price have to be paid. Is from here brethren killing brethren, sistren betraying sistren. Take the knowledge, the blessing, even if the I don't want it, and move on."

Stretching his staff across his chest, Papa Legba raised his arms and exhaled through his mouth, releasing the air from the back of his mouth with a guttural click.

"Hear I words, Benjamin, and mark them well. Follow not the path of the scattered of Israel, they that worshipped Moloch, that sacrificed, that ate their children in return for earthly goods. But follow the path of thy brethren Joseph. Know Babylon works, but never become a bald head."

"Quit the theatrics, Papa Legba. I want to get home and get a good night's sleep."

"If the I don't listen to I, the I sleep will be ever losing."

He lowered his arms and his eyelids clamped shut. His face became contorted and his chest rattled like a broken gourd.

I felt like laughing. I felt so ridiculous lying there on the ground, but Papa Legba wasn't laughing. He was as serious as murder.

He danced around me making a wider and wider circle until he had erased the first circle with his sandal. He placed his staff on my shoulders and then on my head.

"Get up out the mud now, the price is paid," said Papa Legba. "And gird up thy loins. I man sending the I on a mission. Fear not, Benjamin. Jah guide, Jah guide. The I is worthy of the blessings of the Most High."

Another dog came over and licked my heels, my arms then my head.

"Just leave me alone, Papa Legba. Leave me alone. Just let me be!"

"How could the I be anyone but the I," he said, and picked up his staff.

I could feel the staff on my shoulder. It was no use fighting Papa Legba any more. He was right. They, Babylon, had killed or corrupted everything and anyone who was dear to me. If this was to be my blessing, then so be it.

I picked up the bag and Papa Legba was already trodding through the copse in the cool of the night. An armature of stars studded the sky.

CHAPTER TWELVE

When I reached the house, neither Trini nor Cedrick was there. The entire house was fully lit, but no one seemed to be inside. I rang the bell and Jagga emerged from behind the window. I stepped back, but then Emma came to the window, too. When she saw it was me, she opened the front door. She was wearing one of my father's terry-cloth bathrobes, and had her revolver in the pocket.

"Come in quick," she said. "Did you fall? What happened to you?"

Jagga went outside. He called to Butto who came around the corner dragging Tony, hog-tied, along the ground.

"It's not what you think," said Emma. "He'll be all right. David won't hurt him. He promised me."

"Where's Nicole?" I asked. "I thought she was here."

"She's at the guest house. She said you should call her as soon as you get in. She says she'll be waiting by the phone. You need to change that shirt."

"What's she doing there?"

"She went with Chris. Didn't she tell you?"

I felt like someone had kicked a soccer ball into my gut. I didn't want Emma to be worried so I said nothing. We sat in the kitchen, the plastic bag by my feet. I needed to find out all she knew before I acted.

"Are you hungry?" she asked. "Would you like something to drink? Some coffee?"

"No," I said. "I had some patties earlier. I'm not very hungry. What's happening here? What are those guys doing here? Where are our bodyguards?"

"I don't know myself exactly what's happening," she said. "When Trini came back to pick me up, he said Chris needed him at the hotel."

"And Chris left you here alone, unprotected?"

"That's probably why Tony thought he could do whatever he wanted. I caught him rustling around in your room. When I asked him what he was looking for, he tried to attack me, but he never thought I still kept this," and she patted the gun in the robe. "Luckily, Jagga and Butto arrived just then. It was a good thing David sent them here or I don't know if I would have had the nerve to shoot him."

"What was Tony looking for?"

"I don't know," she said, "but I never trusted that boy. He was always sneaking around the house late at night when everybody else had gone to sleep. Spying on everyone for Chris. He must have thought he could do whatever he wanted. Besides, my death wouldn't be a tragedy to anyone."

"It would be for me."

"I didn't mean it that way," she said and touched my face. I winced from the gash in my mouth, but she took it the wrong way.

"I'm sorry," she said. "But you were always so kind to me."

I moved closer to her.

"So what's going to happen to Tony?" I asked, trying to change the subject.

"I'll let David take care of that. I was worried about you. I thought you were hurt."

"Tony was the one who punched me in the mouth."

"Let me see." I opened my mouth and she held my jaw in her hands.

"Poor thing," she said. "Why did he hit you?"

"We were at Verna's..." Then I said, "but let me ask you something."

"Ask me anything."

"Was Albert my father?"

She wasn't prepared for that question. She pulled her hands away and sat down. I showed her the paper. She read it and handed it back to me.

"It got out of hand didn't it?" She tied the belt around her waist. "It began with the most honest of intentions. We wanted to protect your mother."

"My mother? How did she get involved with this?"

"Your mother, Myriam, was the one who started all of this. She's the one who seduced Albert even though she was still married to her first husband, Neville. Myriam and Neville were having a hard time conceiving, so when she told him she was pregnant, he was the happiest man in the world. But six months after you were born, he grew suspicious and somehow found out about Albert and your mother. He was a dead man from then. He drank and stayed out late and when he died in a car accident, nobody was surprised. He was crushed."

"So why didn't she change my name?"

"At first Myriam wouldn't marry Albert, so you kept the name Stewart, at first, to protect Albert's career. We were going to tell you when you were old enough. Albert tried in his own way, but you wouldn't let him. So, I guess, your mother had the ultimate revenge by not telling you the truth. Only me, your mother, Neville and Albert knew differently."

"But why didn't anyone tell me anything all this time – not even my mother when she became a Christian."

"You mean when she became a fanatic!"

"Tell me about it," I said. "I endured so many church services to please her."

"We all endured a lot of things to please her," said Emma. "When she was herself, without her Christianity, she was the kindest, most happy-go-lucky person you would ever want to meet. And the dirty jokes she used to tell!"

"My mother told dirty jokes!"

"Yes," she said and pulled the end of the bathrobe between her legs. "There are some that I couldn't repeat. But after Neville's death, she changed, she became sour. She felt Neville's death was God's punishment and she wouldn't stop until she felt God had punished her enough. That was when she forced Albert out of her bed and into mine. Not that I am proud of it. But I would have done anything for Albert."

"But what about all the other women?"

"I didn't marry him for all the women he slept with," she said. "I married Albert to be with him. And when I found out that I couldn't have any children, it may have been selfish on my part, but I tried to protect you as best as I knew how."

"But people were calling you a leggo beast."

"I've never cared what people called me," she said. "Any woman who stands up for what she wants is called a leggo beast or a whore. Your father was different. And that's why so many women loved him. Me included."

She looked at my shirt again.

"But you, young man, you need to go upstairs and wash. You're filthy. You're meeting your girl friend tomorrow, and you have to look your best. I've left her number by your father's phone in the study."

Emma rose and kissed me on the forehead, "Good night, Jason. You know, if there's anything that you need, any help that I can give you, all you have to do is ask." I kissed her on the cheek. "You know, you don't have to go back to Miami. You could restart the art gallery for me. With your eye, you would have some great paintings on the walls in no time."

She ran her hand across my face, careful not to touch my cheek and said, "Your father really loved you, and he wanted to tell you so many times."

"So why didn't he?"

"Remember when he took you to the airport and he hugged you, that was it!"

"I needed him to say it," I said.

"You're asking too much. Which Jamaican man you know

is going to hug another man in public and tell him he loves him, son or no son?"

She was right; I had been asking too much of him. But shouldn't a son be able to expect everything of his father?

"Good night, Emma," I said, and went into my father's studio. I turned on the light and dialled the number on the paper. The phone rang three times, then clicked, and then rang twice.

"Hello, Nicole? Hello?"

"Hello, Jason." It was Chris. "I was wondering when you would call."

"What's going on, Chris? Is Nicole all right?"

"Your girlfriend is here and she's fine. You know that I wouldn't do anything to hurt her, don't you?"

"Is she all right?"

"Of course, Jason. She's staying in the penthouse suite. I gave it to her for free. I told her nothing was too good for my brother's girlfriend. I've been trying to coax her to go down to the nude section of the beach, but so far she's resisted. Maybe she'll do it for you. She's beautiful."

"You raas," I said. It was like a growl from the bottom of my lungs. In a flash, I thought I'd lost everything.

"C'mon Jason," he said, "that doesn't become you. Anyway let's get down to business. My police friend at Matilda's Corner, after they realized they had to let you go, tell me that your friend told them everything. He says Papa Legba has some papers that belonged to our father. Now, I didn't want you to get involved with this because you're my little brother, you know, but you're going to get the papers from Papa Legba. *How* is your problem. But you better get them."

"Suppose I don't get them. Suppose I can't find him. Papa Legba doesn't obey me. He doesn't obey anyone."

"Oh, you'll find him," he said. "You will. If you don't, your friend will end up in Dovecot for resisting arrest or trying to escape police custody."

I tried to steady my thoughts. It was no use losing my cool. It was like when Reuben and I were playing a soccer match and we were twenty minutes into the second half and down by one goal. We could still win. Me and my idren Reuben would make things right. But I wasn't choosing this battle. Chris was. He was controlling the battlefield, but that didn't mean he would win the war. I had more at stake than he ever realized.

"You wouldn't," I said.

"*I* wouldn't, but the police would. They might get careless, you know."

"Why do you need the papers?" I asked.

"They have some information that I don't want anyone else to have. But we shouldn't be talking about things like that over the phone. You don't know who might be listening."

"Is it the same people with whom our father might have shared the information?"

"Let's get off the topic," he said. "They need those papers that my father got illegally from my bank, otherwise they can't prove anything. But I'm saying too much already. You get the papers."

"But what if they have copies?"

"That's a chance I'll just have to take," he said. "And so what if Washington or anywhere else has copies? I'll play their game. I'll die rich and happy if I don't cross them. You of all people should understand that."

I did. If the next big deposit of iridium were found on his property, Chris would have sold all the mining rights into perpetuity if it meant he could get a million a year and keep his office.

"I'm not coming to meet you unless you're alone," I said. "And unarmed."

I picked up a pen and started doodling on one of the legal pads.

"Of course," he said. I didn't trust him.

"Let me talk with Nicole."

"I'll switch you over right now," he said. "Now, I know I shouldn't need to say this, but please don't say anything to her or Emma about this, or get them to call anyone. I'm monitoring the calls here and Tony is monitoring the calls from the house. Emma's all alone you know."

The phone clicked and then rang twice

"Hello? Hello?" said Nicole.

"Hello, Nicole," I said. "How are you? I thought you'd left. Are you okay?"

"I'm fine," she said. "I was wondering when you were going to call. We have to talk."

"We do," I said. "I'm sorry for being such a bone head."

"We'll have time enough for all of that tomorrow," she said.

So she hadn't deserted me. She hadn't betrayed me as I had betrayed everyone else.

"Are you really okay?"

I was finished with the drawing and signed my name, Jason Lumley, at the bottom of the pad. Son-of-a-bitch or not, he really was my father. I owed him that much.

"Your brother is such a sweetheart! He put me up in this great room and has been treating me like a queen all day. He's so sweet."

"But what are you doing here? I thought you were going back to Miami?"

"After our fight, your brother convinced me that I should stay in Jamaica. He said I shouldn't leave without patching things up. I told Trevor. He left his number on my answering machine."

"He's not in jail?"

"No he's not."

"You're kidding."

"No, I'm not. He convinced the cop's partner that he was on their side and when the medics came, he made sure that they didn't give his partner anything to react with the coke in his system. He said to tell you not to worry about him. He said he couldn't go on living like that. He said that he was going to take the cure and that you'd understand. He's checked himself into a rehab clinic. He says he'll be fine."

At least Trevor had escaped, again. He was safe for now.

"So when will I see you?"

"I'm coming out there tomorrow afternoon."

"I'll be waiting for you," she said and hung up the phone. As I got up from the desk the phone rang. I picked it up.

"If I were you," said Chris, "I wouldn't wait until afternoon. Your boy in jail might not last that long. With the police, you know, anything can happen. Be here by eleven o'clock." And the line went dead.

I turned off the light and went out to the kitchen. I opened the plastic bag and found my father's .38 wrapped in a balance sheet from a bank in the Bahamas. The bag was filled with all kinds of reports, money orders, wire drafts and the plaque.

I couldn't figure it all out, but I knew this was the reason my father was murdered.

CHAPTER THIRTEEN

Morning came in hints of sunlight through the bamboo fronds of Fern Gully as I headed out for the North Coast. I had borrowed Emma's Land Rover, but hadn't told her about my conversation with Chris.

I'd changed into a T-shirt I'd borrowed from Trevor, covered the sofa with a sheet and plopped down until about six o'clock in the morning. I was so angry, I barely slept. Emma scolded me because I hadn't taken a bath and reminded me to drive on the left. She said she knew how it felt to be young and in love, but that I shouldn't take any chances.

And I wasn't. I left a note for Emma that explained what I knew, along with several wire drafts to banks in the Bahamas. I told her that once she'd read the note, she should leave the house with Jagga and go to Carmichael's house. She'd be safe there. She was the only one I could trust with the papers and I left them in a place where I knew she would find them – in the coffee can. By the time she found them, her second pot for the morning, I hoped everything would be over. I didn't want to put her life in danger, and I wasn't sure if Chris had a back up to Tony monitoring the calls from our house. I had to use my wizzy, as Papa Legba said, and do this one alone – I wasn't going to make the same mistake twice.

I kept the rest of the papers, took my father's gun out of the plastic bag and put it in my pants' waist by the small of my back. If Chris had me searched, they probably wouldn't look there because they'd never suspect me of carrying a gun in the first place. Who would suspect a *fenke fenke* man like me to chuck badness? I just had to keep cool.

It was already ten o'clock when I passed Drax Hall and Marcus Garvey's statue outside St. Ann's Bay. A group of girls with branches in their hands were singing "What a Friend I Have in Jesus" as they walked along the side of the road. They had bright red ribbons in their hair, and their starched white dresses and patent leather shoes were brilliant in the morning sun – their lives untouched by the disturbances in Kingston.

Mockingbirds swooped down from the telephone lines and the cedars were a canopy of trills, a descant over the ground swell of organ music from a hilltop church.

Beyond, the imperial crows, aloof to human noise and rubbish, were not yet in sight. As the sun rose over the mountains, the street sounds began: the trundle of jitneys, the squish squish of bicycle tires against the wet asphalt, the tinny squeal of a transistor radio fading into the interminable quarrels of people who waited and waited and waited by bus stops, the street music of lives that crowded the pavement.

The engine surged like the pulse in the pit of my stomach and the blood rushed through my arms and through my knuckles. That was when I realized how hard I'd been holding the steering wheel. My fingers were tingling. Stand firm I told myself, for I could only trust what I was feeling. I only had my head, heart, hands, and feet. I felt naked and confused. Almost as confused as the day when Doc substituted for Basil and decided to teach us a lesson.

Basil's theme all semester had been the value of art and Doc brought with him a print of Vermeer's *Young Woman with a Water Jug* with its exquisite use of light and ingenious use of the window as its source, so that every object in the room – the table, pitcher, bowl, the girl's gown and headdress – was elevated to an image of sanctity. The motionless figures in the room, suspended in time, offered a vision of refuge from the rude world, and a mundane moment of human existence was elevated to a higher plane and captured by the artist for eternity.

But then Doc posed the classic dilemma of a fire in a museum and the choice between an old lady and this Vermeer. I convinced the rest of the class – I was sure Basil would have agreed with me – to save the Vermeer. The old lady, I argued, was already on her way out, her molecules of nitrogen, carbon, and calcium would soon join the clay on the cricket mound. But the Vermeer was priceless and had to be preserved at all costs.

But now I wasn't too sure. Every value I'd cherished and remembered had met its opposite and had been cancelled. Justice would have demanded another course than the one that was now leading me to a direct collision with my brother, Chris – a course I had never desired or wished for – but it was inevitable. But what was Justice without a human face? Reuben and Nicole were worth more to me than a million Vermeers. The Old Dutch Massa could burn in hell any day. I'd take Nicole's or Verna's face for all he could ever paint.

As I came over the hill and descended to the coastline, the road was littered with dead crabs. During the night, careless and excited by the gentle squall that had whipped through the leaves of the sea grapes, they had thrown themselves heedlessly into the lights of oncoming cars. The wheels had crunched down on their stony armour and splintered their shells before burying them in the mud.

For a moment I felt bewildered, like a traveller who knows the history and geography of the desired destination, who knows from a map the contours of a coastline, but when faced with the reality, a headland receding into the horizon, is consumed by breathlessness.

The sky was blue, smoke was rising off a nearby hill, but I didn't care. I only wanted to see Nicole. I turned on the radio to take my mind off things. Bob was singing "One

Love". I drove along with the music, going up and down the country roads clearing my mind for whatever I would confront on the road ahead.

When I got to the gates of Anastasia's, a little boy in ragged clothes directed me towards the parking lot. The hotel, a series of white bungalows with shingled roofs surrounded by a restaurant, bar and lobby, dominated the headland.

Circling the parking lot, I looked down the hill for Chris. He was there, alone. So far, so good. He had kept that part of the bargain. But that didn't mean anything.

I parked by a hedge that shielded the changing rooms and took the plastic bag out of the jeep, and put on my jacket to make sure the gun was hidden. I was ready for anything.

Past the restaurant and pool, a bamboo fence that enclosed the hotel grounds from the stark cliffs ran erratically down the northern slope of the hillside. A black man was leading some pink people down a rocky path to the beach. The sea was on fire.

Chris was waiting for me near a boulder that marked the entrance to the limestone caves that were a favourite tourist attraction because of the deep grottoes, the seemingly bottomless pools and the stream that connected to the Roaring River.

I looked again to see if Chris was really alone before I went any further. Should I just shoot him now when I had the chance, I asked myself. Why had it come to this?

"I see you have the papers," he said. I couldn't see any sign that he was carrying a gun. He twirled a walkie-talkie from a string.

"Where's Nicole?" I asked, barely containing my anger.

"She's in her room," he said. "After you give me the papers, I'll call Trini and he'll come down with her. You can spend the rest of the afternoon here on the beach and leave tonight. Jason, this is not your fight any more. I could kill you right here and no one would care. But you're my brother and I don't have any bad feelings towards you, so I'm going to ask you to leave. I've already confirmed your flight.

But always remember, I can always get to you."

I didn't trust Chris, but there was nothing I could do. I played along with him because he could have killed me as I came down the path.

"What about Adrian?"

"I'll call Cedrick and tell him to relay the message to the police. He'll get away."

A muffled sound, the sea rising up through the underground streams on the promontory, tumbled out of the mouth of the cave.

"How do I know, you won't have him killed once you get the papers from me."

"Jason, I'm your brother. I've never lied to you before, and I'll never lie to you. I know you never liked Dada any more than I did and you obviously don't want to stay here in Jamaica. You're no real threat to me, so once I get the papers, he will get away. I promise you."

"I don't trust you, Chris," and I think he heard the fury in my voice.

"What choice do you have, Jason?" he said calmly.

"So why did you kill him, Chris?"

"It was self-defence, Jason. It was me or him. He was bound to get me sooner or later. Better him than me."

I shrugged my shoulders and walked towards him with the bag of papers. I was about ten feet away from him when I heard, "Don't dweet, Jah-son. Don't trade your birthright for the poison of Satan."

Papa Legba was standing behind Chris at the entrance of the caves. I was never happier to see that old dread. Give thanks, old dread, I whispered under my breath, for although I thought I'd readied myself with my own talk, I really didn't know what I was going to do. I needed his help.

"Papa Legba, Rasta," I said and backed away.

"I and I in control," said Papa Legba. "You brethren dead already. Him free as the day him born."

Reuben, my brethren, my idren, dead?

"You old fucker!" screamed Chris, and pulled out a gun

from inside his shirt. I pulled Dada's gun from my back. He had already killed Dada and Adrian, kidnapped Nicole, and now he was going to kill Papa Legba. Brother or no brother, his ruthlessness had to be stopped, for all our sakes. I pulled out the gun and fired.

"You shot me, Jason, you shot me," he said and grabbed his side. He seemed more amazed than angry.

"Your own brother and you shot me." He spun wildly, his face wrinkled with pain, his hand flailing in the air, but he managed to get off a shot before he fell to the ground. He shot Papa Legba.

Papa Legba fell to the ground, gripping his chest. I ran over to Chris, kicked his gun away, and then put it in my waist. Chris was cursing up a storm, pure bumbo, raas, and claat. I went over to Papa Legba's side and held his head in my lap. He was going fast.

"Dread, dread, you can't leave me like this. You can't die." My father's gun felt warm and heavy all of a sudden and I rested it on the ground.

"I and I was never here," he said, confusing me to the end. "I and I don't dead. I going to life. When I reach Mount Zion, Enoch will say to I, 'Leroy, the I shall inherit the crown of life ever-living. The I run the good race. Inherit the kingdom of thy father.' I and I will be one…"

And then he closed his eyes, slowly mumbling some words that I couldn't understand until his voice sounded as if it was coming from a far away place. Then the noise stopped. Everything was quiet except for the sea.

I pulled him under the shade and checked on Chris. He was still alive. My hands were still shaking as I went down to the hotel to call the police. I hid the guns inside my jacket and glanced over my shoulder to check them before I went inside the hotel. The turquoise blue waters of the Caribbean almost blinded me. A hibiscus bled from the fence.

As I went into the front door of the hotel, I was shocked by my own reflection in the mirrors of the hotel's lobby. In the middle of the lobby, a cedar totem pole sprouted the head of a Rastaman whose locks became the features of other faces below him and crowned the trunk.

The fans facing the restaurant, their blades painted red, green, and gold, turned lazily and a wily philodendron snaked up the right side of the restaurant and across the ceiling, wrapping itself around the track lights.

I dialled the number, and looked down to the beach at the happy people who were tanning in the sun and feeding the gulls, whose eyes were fixed on the slivers of bread, like the children who were barred from the hotel's entrance.

I called the operator to see if I could contact Nicole in the penthouse suite. She said there was no answer, but she would try again. As I held the phone, I looked down at the Tiki huts that dotted the promontory. At the furthest end of the beach, Nicole was sitting under a palm tree. She was wearing a tangerine bikini and sipping a green drink that only a tourist would buy.

A waitress passed by her and gave her a look that meant no self-respecting Jamaican woman, and especially on a Sunday morning, should be seen in public wearing something like that. Nicole ignored her and shifted the straw hat on her head.

The police were on their way. I ran down to the beach and surprised her as she dabbed sun tan lotion on her thighs.

"Nicole!"

"I've been waiting for you," she said innocently, and dried her arms with a towel.

I didn't want to speak any more. I didn't want her to speak. I only wanted to taste her salt mouth, her smooth skin.

I kissed her and held her and kissed her and held her, knocking the straw hat off her head.

"How did you know I was down here?" I asked when I finally let her go.

"An old Rastaman came up to my room. He whispered something to the man who was outside my door, and the guy took off. Then he told me to meet you here. He said you would understand," she said, picking up the hat and putting a stone on the brim so it wouldn't blow away.

"That old rascal."

"Who?"

"Papa Legba, of course."

Police cars were coming up the hill. I held Nicole's hand as we went down to the field, the sandy soil slipping under our feet, towards the mouth of the cave.

There, it looked as if an anthill had been crushed by a careless forager. The paramedics buzzed around like determined workers and hustled Chris into the ambulance. He'd gone into shock and was now unconscious. The police had covered Papa Legba's body.

I greeted the detective in charge and shook his hand. He was a medium-built, broad-shouldered man whose military gait and style commanded the respect of the other policemen, and they responded to the slightest movement of his fingers.

"Hello, my name is Jason Lumley, Albert Lumley's son," I said, turning on the air of authority that I'd learned from Papa Legba, Carmichael, Doc, and my father, but in my own tone. I'd recovered my voice. "I returned from Miami to take over my father's affairs when this awful tragedy occurred."

The detective looked me over. He shook my hand cautiously, then took a statement from me. Through it all Nicole caressed my shoulders and rubbed my nape. She gripped my hand, especially when she heard about Chris eavesdropping on our conversation over the phone, and when she realized that she had been kidnapped.

"I need to get away from here, fast," she said.

"Take it easy," I said. "I'm here."

"Are you really?" she asked. From the way I'd behaved before, I guess she had every right to ask me that question.

"I am," I replied and put my hand around her waist. At first she pulled away. I couldn't blame her, I'd just shot a man, my own brother.

"Nicole, please, stand firm beside me," I said and beckoned to her.

"I've stood firm beside you from the start, Jason. From the start."

The detective broke in and said, "You know you cyaan leave the island until the investigation is over."

"That means I'll have to quit my job in Miami," I said. Nicole kissed me on the cheek and whispered in my ear, "I need to go down to the beach and wash all of this away."

I didn't want to let her go.

The policeman closed his pad and said, "From what you've told me, Mr. Lumley, you'll probably won't face charges. We'll take the bag in as evidence. I'll see you in Kingston in a week or so."

I took hold of Nicole's hand firmly, then released her when she pulled away. But then gently, slowly, she came back and stood by my side.

"You know," she said "I should be angry with you for keeping all of this from me, like I couldn't take the heat."

"You should," I said. "You have every right, Nicole."

She looked at me hard, then nodded her head as if she sensed something new in my voice. She was right.

"I know this may seem out of order," I said turning to the police officer, "but how do I know this evidence won't disappear?"

The detective smiled at me, then said, "Your father had me working on the case. And Mrs. Lumley call ahead and make sure is me get the call and not anybody else or else you would have ended up with a sure gun charge. I had to make sure everything was straight for the record," he said aloud so everyone could hear and he walked away.

"So what are you going to do now?" said Nicole anxiously. She dug her toes into the sand.

"I don't know yet, but I have to go and look for Reuben's kids in Kingston. But the first thing I'm going to do is take a bathe. I stink."

"You do," said Nicole and she looked up at me. "But don't go alone. Let me walk with you. Let me get my hat first," and she ran down to the beach.

As she ran, she frightened a flock of gulls that lifted themselves into the air. The gulls spiralled up towards the clouds, a column of feathers that, for a second, blotted out the sun. They circled the beach in widening concentric arcs, then came in low behind the tide.

I watched Nicole as she picked up her hat, turned and came back to me with her sure, steady gait. In the sureness of her presence, I surrendered. There was no need to run any more. I was home.

I followed her naked waist into the sea.

Geoffrey Philp was born in rural Struie in Jamaica. Like his near contemporary Kwame Dawes he attended Jamaica College.

He is the author of four poetry collections, *Exodus and Other Poems*, *Florida Bound*, *hurricane center*, and *xango music*. He has also written a book of short stories, *Uncle Obadiah and the Alien*. *Benjamin, My Son* is his first novel.

A recipient of many awards for his work, including an Individual Artist Fellowship from the Florida Arts Council, The Sauza Stay Pure Award, James Michener fellowships at the University of Miami, and an artist-in-residence at the Seaside Institute, he is currently working on a new collection of short stories, *Sister Faye and the Dreadlocked Vampire*. "The River" which appears in *Uncle Obadiah and the Alien*, won the Canute Brodhurst Prize from *The Caribbean Writer*. Philp's poems and short stories have also appeared in *Asili*, *The Mississippi Review*, *The Caribbean Writer*, *Gulf Stream*, *The Apalachee Quarterly*, *Journal of Caribbean Studies*, *Florida in Poetry*, *Wheel and Come Again: An Anthology of Reggae Poetry*, *The Oxford Book of Caribbean Short Stories*, and most recently, *Whispers from the Cotton Tree Root*.

OTHER BOOKS BY GEOFFREY PHILP

Uncle Obadiah and the Alien

How does an alien with an unfortunate resemblance to Margaret Thatcher come to be in Uncle Obadiah's yard smoking all his best weed? This beautifully crafted and frequently hilarious collection of short stories is guaranteed to lift even the deepest gloom. Written in Jamaican patois and standard English, this is a brilliant read which will lead you through the yards of Jamaica to the streets of Miami. Here is a contemporary world, warts and all. Geoffrey Philp goes beyond stereotypes to portray the individuality and humanity in all his characters. And of course there is always the best lamb's breath colly to help improve the day.

Robert Antoni writes: 'If Dickens were reincarnated as a Jamaican Rastaman, he would write stories as hilarious and humane as these. "Uncle Obadiah" and the other stories collected here announce Geoffrey Philp as a direct descendent of Bob Marley: poet, philosophizer, spokesperson for our next new world.'

John Dufresne writes: 'Geoffrey Philp is a literary shaman, an enchanter, a weaver of spells that reveal unexpected and marvelous things about life, that carry the news of island culture to the mainland. From the first word of the first story in this comic and touching collection, Philp lifts me out of my world and drops me into the world of his charming, beleaguered and compelling characters. *Uncle Obadiah and the Alien* is one of those rare treasures, a book you can't put down and won't ever forget.'

ISBN: 1-900715-01-5
Pages: 160
Published: 01 February 1997
£6.99

Florida Bound

These poems of exasperation and longing explore a reluctance to leave Jamaica and the 'marl-white roads at Struie' and anger that 'blackman still can't live in him own/black land' where 'gunman crawl like bedbug'. But whilst poems explore the keeness and sorrows of an exile's memory, the new landscape of South Florida landscape fully engages the poet's imagination. The experience of journeying is seen as part of a larger pattern of restless but creative movement in the Americas. Philp joins other Caribbean poets in making use of nation language, but few have pushed the collision between roots language and classical forms to greater effect.

Carrol Fleming writes in *The Caribbean Writer*: 'His poems are as vibrant and diverse as Miami where "each street crackles with dialects/variegated as the garish crotons". Miami, albeit citified, becomes just one more island with all that is good, bad and potentially violent beset by the same sea, same hurricanes, and "mangroves lashed sapless by the wind".

"Philp's poems wander through bedrooms and along the waterfronts of that perceptive land accessible only to poets, only to those who can pull the day through dawn fog to the delicate "breath of extinguished candles".

"Philp weaves dialect and landscape into his lines with subtle authority. It is easy to get caught up in the content and miss the grace of his technique."

ISBN: 0-948833-82-3
Pages: 64
Published: 01 April 1995
Price: £5.95

Hurricane center

El nino stirs clouds over the Pacific. Flashing TV screens
urge a calm that no one believes. The police beat a slouched
body, crumpled like a fist of kleenex. The news racks are
crowded with stories of pestilence, war and rumours of
war. The children, once sepia-faced cherubim, mutate to
monsters that eat, eat, eat. You notice a change in your
body's conversation with itself, and in the garden the fire
ants burrow into the flesh of the fruit.

Geoffrey Philps's poems stare into the dark heart of a
world where hurricanes, both meteorological and meta-
phorical, threaten you to the last cell. But the sense of dread
also reveals what is most precious in life, for the dark and
accidental are put in the larger context of season and human
renewal, and *Hurricane Center* returns always to the possibilities of redemption and joy.

In the voices of Jamaican prophets, Cuban exiles, exotic
dancers, drunks, race-track punters, canecutters, rastamen,
middle-class householders and screw-face ghetto sufferers,
Geoffrey Philp writes poetry which is both intimately
human and cosmic in scale. On the airwaves between Miami
and Kingston, the rhythms of reggae and mambo dance
through these poems.

ISBN: 1-900715-23-6
Pages: 67
Published: 01 February 1998
Price: £6.99

In the Xango ceremony, the contraries of New World African experience find transcendence. From the established, bodily patterns of ritual comes release into the freedom of the spirit; from the exposure of pain comes the possibilities of healing; and for the individual there is both the dread aloneness with the gods and the 'we-ness' of community.

Simultaneously the rites celebrate the rich, syncretic diversity, the multiple connections of the African person in the New World and enact the tragic search for the wholeness of the lost African centre. And there is the god himself, standing at the crossroads, 'beating iron into the shape of thunder', both the prophetic voice warning of the fire to command the creator who hammers out sweet sound from the iron drum.

Geoffrey Philp finds in Xango a powerful metaphor that is both particular to the Caribbean and universal in its relevance.

David and Phyllis Gershator writes in *The Caribbean Writer*: 'Using rhythm and riffs, he can pull the stops on language and give it a high energy kick. In 'jam-rock' he winds up with 'the crack of bones, the sweat of the whip; girl, you gonna get a lot of it; get it galore; my heart still beats uncha, uncha uncha, cha'(31).

ISBN: 1-900715-46-5
Pages: 64
Published: 01 June 2001
Price: £6.99

Kwame Dawes
A Place to Hide

A man lies in a newspaper-lined room dreaming an other life. Bob Marley's spirit flew into him at the moment of the singer's death. A woman detaches herself from her perfunctory husband and finds the erotic foreplay she longs for in journeying round the island. A man climbs Blue Mountain Peak to fly and hear the voice of God. Sonia paints her new friend Joan and hopes that this will be the beginning of a sexual adventure.

Dawes's characters are driven by their need for intimate contact with people and with God, and their need to construct personal myths powerful enough to live by. In a host of distinctive and persuasive voices they tell stories that reveal their inner lives and give an incisive portrayal of contemporary Jamaican society that is unsparing in confronting its elements of misogyny and nihilistic violence.

Indeed several stories question how this disorder can be meaningfully told without either sensationalism or despair. For Dawes, the answer is found in the creative energies that lie just the other side of chaos. In particular, in the dub vershan episodes, which intercut the stories, there are intense and moving celebrations of moments of reggae creation in the studio and in performance.

Kwame Dawes has established a growing international reputation as a poet and these are stories that combine a poetic imagination with narrative drive, an acute social awareness and a deep inwardness in the treatment of character. In the penultimate story, 'Marley's Ghost', Dawes's imagination soars to towering myth.

ISBN: 1-900715-48-1
Pages: 312
Published: 01 March 2003
Price: £9.99

Peepal Tree Press publishes a wide selection of outstanding fiction, poetry, drama, history and literary criticism with a focus on the Caribbean, Africa, the South Asian diaspora and Black life in Britain. Peepal Tree is now the largest independent publisher of Caribbean writing in the world. All our books are high quality original paperbacks designed to stand the test of time and repeated readings.

All Peepal Tree books should be available through your local bookseller, though you are even more welcome to place orders direct with us on the Peepal Tree website and on-line bookstore: www.peepaltreepress.com. You can also order direct by phone or in writing.

Peepal Tree sends out regular e-mail information about new books and special offers. We also produce a yearly catalogue which gives current prices in sterling, US and Canadian dollars and full details of all our books. Contact us to join our mailing list.

You can contact Peepal Tree at:

17 King's Avenue
Leeds LS6 1QS
United Kingdom

e-mail hannah@peepaltreepress.com
tel: 44 (0)113 245 1703

website: www.peepaltreepress.com